The Author

DUNCAN CAMPBELL SCOTT was born in Ottawa, Ontario, in 1862. He was educated there and at Stanstead College in Quebec. He entered the civil service in 1879 as a junior clerk in what would become the Department of Indian Affairs; by 1913 he had risen to the rank of Deputy Superintendent General, a position he held until his retirement in 1932.

Urged to write by his close friend Archibald Lampman, Scott became a skilled and popular poet, short-story writer, and casual essayist. His best-known stories, such as those collected in *In the Village of Viger* (1896), are delicate yet intense explorations of traditional communities and cultures struggling to adjust to a rapidly changing world. His poetry often reflects his concerns for and sympathy with the lives of Native peoples.

Duncan Campbell Scott died in Ottawa in 1947.

Duncan Campbell Scott

IN THE VILLAGE
OF VIGER

With an Afterword by Tracy Ware

M&S

The following note appeared in the original edition:

*I am indebted to Messrs. Charles Scribner's Sons for
permission to reprint several of these tales.*

D.C.S.

Copyright © 1996 by McClelland & Stewart Ltd.
Afterword copyright © 1996 by Tracy Ware

In the Village of Viger was first published in 1896 by Copeland and Day,
Boston. "The Return," which first appeared in *Massey's Magazine*
(November 1896), and "Coquelicot," which first appeared in the Christmas
1901 number of *The Globe*, are reprinted from *The Circle of Affection and
Other Pieces in Prose and Verse* (McClelland and Stewart, 1947).

New Canadian Library edition 1996

National Library of Canada Cataloguing in Publication

Scott, Duncan Campbell, 1862-1947
In the village of Viger

(New Canadian library)
First ed. published under title: In the village of Viger and other stories.
Includes bibliographical references.
ISBN 0-7710-3460-1

I. Title. II. Series

PS8537.C5815 1996   C813'.4   C96-930385-8
PR9199.3.S3315 1996

We acknowledge the financial support of the Government of Canada
through the Book Publishing Industry Development Program and
that of the Government of Ontario through the Ontario Media
Development Corporation's Ontario Book Initiative. We further
acknowledge the support of the Canada Council for the Arts and the
Ontario Arts Council for our publishing program.

Typesetting by M&S, Toronto

Printed and bound in Canada

McClelland & Stewart Ltd.
The Canadian Publishers
481 University Avenue
Toronto, Ontario
M5G 2E9
www.mcclelland.com/NCL

2 3 4 5 6   07 06 05 04 03

To my daughter
Elizabeth Duncan Scott

Robins and bobolinks bubbling and tinkling,
    Shore-larks alive there high in the blue,
Level in the sunlight the rye-field twinkling,
    The wind parts the cloud and a star leaps through,
Ferns at the spring-head curling cool and tender,
    Bloodroot in the tangle, violets by the larch,
In the dusky evening the young moon slender,
    Glowing like a crocus in the dells of March;
All a world of music, of laughter, and of lightness,
    Crushed to a diamond, rounded to a pearl,
Moulded to a flower bell, – cannot match the brightness
    In the darling beauty of one sweet girl.

Whoever has from toil and stress
Put into ports of idleness,
And watched the gleaming thistledown
Wheel in the soft air lazily blown;
Or leaning on the shady rail,
Beneath the poplars, silver pale,
Eyed in the shallow amber pools
The black perch voyaging in schools;
Or heard the fisherman outpour
His strange and questionable lore,
While the cream-blossomed basswood-trees
Boomed like an organ with the bees;
Or by blind fancy held aloof
Has startled with prosaic hoof,
Beneath the willows in the shade,
The wooing of a pretty maid;
And traced the sharp or genial air
Of human nature everywhere:
Might find perchance the wandered fire,
Around St. Joseph's sparkling spire;
And wearied with the fume and strife,
The complex joys and ills of life,
Might for an hour his worry staunch,
In pleasant Viger by the Blanche.

Contents

The Little Milliner   3
The Desjardins   15
The Wooing of Monsieur Cuerrier   21
Sedan   30
No. 68 Rue Alfred de Musset   39
The Bobolink   50
The Tragedy of the Seigniory   55
Josephine Labrosse   66
The Pedler   74
Paul Farlotte   79

APPENDIX

The Return   93
Coquelicot   104

Afterword   119

In the Village of Viger

The Little Milliner

IT WAS TOO true that the city was growing rapidly. As yet its arms were not long enough to embrace the little village of Viger, but before long they would be, and it was not a time that the inhabitants looked forward to with any pleasure. It was not to be wondered at, for few places were more pleasant to live in. The houses, half-hidden amid the trees, clustered around the slim steeple of St. Joseph's, which flashed like a naked poniard in the sun. They were old, and the village was sleepy, almost dozing, since the mill, behind the rise of land, on the Blanche had shut down. The miller had died; and who would trouble to grind what little grist came to the mill, when flour was so cheap? But while the beech-groves lasted, and the Blanche continued to run, it seemed impossible that any change could come. The change was coming, however, rapidly enough. Even now, on still nights, above the noise of the frogs in the pools, you could hear the rumble of the street-cars and the faint tinkle of their bells, and when the air was moist the whole southern sky was luminous with the reflection of thousands of gas-lamps. But when the time came for Viger to be mentioned in the city papers as one of the outlying wards, what a change there would be! There would be no unfenced fields, full of little inequalities and covered with short grass; there would be no deep pools, where the quarries had been, and where the boys pelted the frogs; there would be no more beech-groves, where the children could gather nuts; and the dread pool, which had filled the shaft where old Daigneau, years ago, mined for gold, would cease to exist. But in the meantime, the boys of Viger roamed over the unclosed fields and pelted the frogs, and the boldest ventured to roll huge stones into Daigneau's pit, and only waited to see the green slime come working up to the surface before scampering away, their flesh creeping with the idea that it was old Daigneau himself who was stirring up the water in a rage.

New houses had already commenced to spring up in all directions, and there was a large influx of the laboring population which overflows from large cities. Even on the main street of Viger, on a lot which had been vacant ever since it was a lot, the workmen had built a foundation. After a while it was finished, when men from the city came and put up the oddest wooden house that one could imagine. It was perfectly square; there was a window and a door in front, a window at the side, and a window upstairs. There were many surmises as to the probable occupant of such a diminutive habitation; and the widow Laroque, who made dresses and trimmed hats, and whose shop was directly opposite, and next door to the Post Office, suffered greatly from unsatisfied curiosity. No one who looked like the proprietor was ever seen near the place. The foreman of the laborers who were working at the house seemed to know nothing; all that he said, in answer to questions, was: "I have my orders."

At last the house was ready; it was painted within and without, and Madame Laroque could scarcely believe her eyes when, one morning, a man came from the city with a small sign under his arm and nailed it above the door. It bore these words: "Mademoiselle Viau, Milliner." "Ah!" said Madame Laroque, "the bread is to be taken out of my mouth." The next day came a load of furniture, – not a very large load, as there was only a small stove, two tables, a bedstead, three chairs, a sort of lounge, and two large boxes. The man who brought the things put them in the house, and locked the door on them when he went away; then nothing happened for two weeks, but Madame Laroque watched. Such a queer little house it was, as it stood there so new in its coat of gum-colored paint. It looked just like a square bandbox which some Titan had made for his wife; and there seemed no doubt that if you took hold of the chimney and lifted the roof off, you would see the gigantic bonnet, with its strings and ribbons, which the Titaness could wear to church on Sundays.

Madame Laroque wondered how Mademoiselle Viau would come, whether in a cab, with her trunks and boxes piled around her, or on foot, and have her belongings on a cart. She watched every approaching vehicle for two weeks in vain; but one morning she saw that a curtain had been put up on the window opposite, that it was partly raised, and that a geranium was standing on the sill. For one hour she never took her eyes off the door, and at last had the satisfaction of seeing it open. A trim little person, not very young, dressed in gray, stepped out on the platform with her apron full of crumbs and cast them down for the birds. Then, without looking around, she went in and closed the door. It was Mademoiselle Viau. "The bird is in its nest," thought the old postmaster, who lived alone with his mother. All that Madame Laroque said was: "Ah!"

Mademoiselle Viau did not stir out that day, but on the next she went to the baker's and the butcher's, and came over the road to Monsieur Cuerrier, the postmaster, who also kept a grocery.

That evening, according to her custom, Madame Laroque called on Madame Cuerrier.

"We have a neighbor," she said.

"Yes."

"She was making purchases to-day."

"Yes."

"To-morrow she will expect people to make purchases."

"Without doubt."

"It is very tormenting, this, to have these irresponsible girls, that no one knows anything about, setting up shops under our very noses. Why does she live alone?"

"I did not ask her," answered Cuerrier, to whom the question was addressed.

"You are very cool, Monsieur Cuerrier; but if it was a young man and a postmaster, instead of a young woman and a milliner, you would not relish it."

"There can be only one postmaster," said Cuerrier.

"In Paris, where I practised my art," said Monsieur Villeblanc, who was a retired hairdresser, "there were whole rows of tonsorial parlors, and every one had enough to do." Madame Laroque sniffed, as she always did in his presence.

"Did you see her hat?" she asked.

"I did, and it was very nice."

"Nice! with the flowers all on one side? I wouldn't go to St. Thérèse with it on." St. Thérèse was the postmaster's native place.

"The girl has no taste," she continued.

"Well, if she hasn't, you needn't be afraid of her."

"There will be no choice between you," said the retired hairdresser, maliciously.

But there was a choice between them, and all the young girls of Viger chose Mademoiselle Viau. It was said she had such an eye; she would take a hat and pin a bow on here, and loop a ribbon there, and cast a flower on somewhere else, all the time surveying her work with her head on one side and her mouth bristling with pins. "There, how do you like that? – put it on – no, it is not becoming – wait!" and in a trice the desired change was made. She had no lack of work from the first; soon she had too much to do. At all hours of the day she could be seen sitting at her window, working, and "she must be making money fast," argued Madame Laroque, "for she spends nothing." In truth, she spent very little – she lived so plainly. Three times a week she took a fresh twist from the baker, once a day the milkman left a pint of milk, and once every week mademoiselle herself stepped out to the butcher's and bought a pound of steak. Occasionally she mailed a letter, which she always gave into the hands of the postmaster; if he was not there she asked for a pound of tea or something else that she needed. She was fast friends with Cuerrier, but with no one else, as she never received visitors. Once only did a young man call on her. It was young Jourdain, the clerk in the dry-goods store. He had knocked at the door and was admitted. "Ah!" said Madame Laroque, "it is the young men who can conquer." But the next moment Monsieur Jourdain came out, and, strangely enough, was so bewildered as to forget to put on his hat. It was not this young man who could conquer.

"There is something mysterious about that young person," said Madame Laroque between her teeth.

"Yes," replied Cuerrier, "very mysterious – she minds her own business."

"Bah!" said the widow, "who can tell what her business is, she who comes from no one knows where? But I'll find out what all this secrecy means, trust me!"

So the widow watched the little house and its occupant very closely, and these are some of the things she saw: Every morning an open door and crumbs for the birds, the watering of the geranium, which was just going to flower, a small figure going in and out, dressed in gray, and, oftener than anything else, the same figure sitting at the window, working. This continued for a year with little variation, but still the widow watched. Every one else had accepted the presence of the new resident as a benefaction. They had got accustomed to her. They called her "the little milliner." Old Cuerrier called her "the little one in gray." But she was not yet adjusted in the widow's system of things. She laid a plot with her second cousin, which was that the cousin should get a hat made by Mademoiselle Viau, and that she should ask her some questions.

"Mademoiselle Viau, were you born in the city?"

"I do not think, Mademoiselle, that green will become you."

"No, perhaps not. Where did you live before you came here?"

"Mademoiselle, this gray shape is very pretty." And so on. That plan would not work.

But before long something very suspicious happened. One evening, just about dusk, as Madame Laroque was walking up and down in front of her door, a man of a youthful appearance came quickly up the street, stepped upon Mademoiselle Viau's platform, opened the door without knocking, and walked in. Mademoiselle was working in the last vestige of daylight, and the widow watched her like a lynx. She worked on unconcernedly, and when it became so dark that she could not see she lit her lamp and pulled down the curtain. That night Madame Laroque did not go into Cuerrier's. It commenced to rain, but she put on a large frieze coat of the deceased Laroque and crouched in the dark. She was very much interested in this case, but her interest brought no additional knowledge. She had seen the man go in; he was rather young and about the medium height, and had a black mustache; she could remember him distinctly, but she did not see him come out.

The next morning Mademoiselle Viau's curtain went up as usual, and as it was her day to go to the butcher's she went out. While she was away Madame Laroque took a long look in at the side window, but there was nothing to see except the lounge and the table.

While Madame Laroque had been watching in the rain, Cuerrier was reading to Villeblanc from *Le Monde*. "Hello!" said he, and then went on reading to himself.

"Have you lost your voice?" asked Villeblanc, getting nettled.

"No, no; listen to this – 'Daring Jewel Robbery. A Thief in the Night.'" These were the headings of the column, and then followed the particulars. In the morning the widow borrowed the paper, as she had been too busy the night before to come and hear it read. She looked over the front page, when her eye caught the heading, "Daring Jewel Robbery," and she read the whole story. As she neared the end her eyebrows commenced to travel up her forehead, as if they were going to hide in her hair, and with an expression of surprise she tossed the paper to her second cousin.

"Look here!" she said, "read this out to me."

The second cousin commenced to read at the top.

"No, no! right here."

"'The man Durocher, who is suspected of the crime, is not tall, wears a heavy mustache, has gray eyes, and wears an ear-ring in his left ear. He has not been seen since Saturday.'"

"I told you so!" exclaimed the widow.

"You told me nothing of the kind," said the second cousin.

"He had no ear-ring in his ear," said the widow – "but – but – but it was the *right* ear that I saw. Hand me my shawl!"

"Where are you going?"

"I have business; never mind!" She took the paper with her and went straight to the constable.

"But," said he, "I cannot come."

"There is no time to be lost; you must come now."

"But he will be desperate; he will face me like a lion."

"Never mind! you will have the reward."

"Well, wait!" And the constable went upstairs to get his pistol.

He came down with his blue coat on. He was a very fat man, and was out of breath when he came to the little milliner's.

"But who shall I ask for?" he inquired of Madame Laroque.

"Just search the house, and I will see that he does not escape by the back door." She had forgotten that there was no back door.

"Do you want a bonnet?" asked Mademoiselle Viau. She was on excellent terms with the constable.

"No!" said he, sternly. "You have a man in this house, and I have come to find him."

"Indeed?" said mademoiselle, very stiffly. "Will you be pleased to proceed?"

"Yes," said he, taking out his pistol and cocking it. "I will first look downstairs." He did so, and only frightened a cat from under the stove. No one knew that Mademoiselle Viau had a cat.

"Lead the way upstairs!" commanded the constable.

"I am afraid of your pistol, will you not go first?"

He went first and entered at once the only room, for there was no hall. In the mean time Madame Laroque had found out that there was no back door, and had come into the lower flat and reinspected it, looking under everything.

"Open that closet!" said the constable, as he levelled his pistol at the door.

Mademoiselle threw open the door and sprang away, with her hands over her ears. There was no one there; neither was there any one under the bed.

"Open that trunk!" eying the little leather-covered box.

"Monsieur, you will respect – but – as you will." She stooped over the trunk and threw back the lid; on the top was a dainty white skirt, embroidered beautifully. The little milliner was blushing violently.

"That will do!" said the constable. "There is no one there."

"Get out of the road!" he cried to the knot of people who had collected at the door. "I have been for my wife's bonnet; it is not finished." But the people looked at his pistol, which he had forgotten to put away. He went across to the widow's.

"Look here!" he said, "you had better stop this or I'll have the law on you – no words now! Making a fool of me before the people – getting me to put on my coat and bring my pistol to frighten a cat from under the stove. No words now!"

"Monsieur Cuerrier," inquired Madame Laroque that night, "who is it that Mademoiselle Viau writes to?"

"I am an official of the government. I do not tell state secrets."

"State secrets, indeed! Depend upon it, there are secrets in those letters which the state would like to know."

"That is not my business. I only send the letters where they are posted, and refuse to tell amiable widows where they go."

The hairdresser, forgetting his constant fear of disarranging his attire, threw back his head and laughed wildly.

"Trust a barber to laugh," said the widow. Villeblanc sobered up and looked sadly at Cuerrier; he could not bear to be called a barber.

"And you uphold her in this – a person who comes from no one knows where, and writes to no one knows who —"

"I know who she writes to —" The widow got furious.

"Yes, who she writes to – yes, of course you do – that person who comes out of her house without ever having gone into it, and who is visited by men who go in and never come out —"

"How do you know he went in?"

"I saw him."

"How do you know he never came out?"

"I didn't see him."

"Ah! then you were watching?"

"Well, what if I was! The devil has a hand in it."

"I have no doubt," said Cuerrier, insinuatingly.

"Enough, fool!" exclaimed the widow – "but wait, I have not done yet!"

"You had better rest, or you will have the law on you."

The widow was afraid of the law.

About six months after this, when the snow was coming on, a messenger came from the city with a telegram for Monsieur Cuerrier – at least, it was in his care. He very seldom went out, but he got his boots and went across to Mademoiselle Viau's. The telegram was for her. When she had read it she crushed it in her hand and leaned against the wall. But she recovered herself.

"Monsieur Cuerrier, you have always been a good friend to me – help me! I must go away – you will watch my little place when I am gone!"

The postmaster was struck with pity, and he assisted her. She left that night.

"*Accomplice!*" the widow hissed in his ear the first chance she got.

About three weeks after this, when Madame Laroque asked for *Le Monde*, Cuerrier refused to give it to her.

"Where is it?"

"It has been lost."

"*Lost!*" said the widow, derisively. "Well, I will find it." In an hour she came back with the paper.

"There!" said she, thrusting it under the postmaster's nose so that he could not get his pipe back to his mouth. Cuerrier looked consciously at the paragraph which she had pointed out. He had seen it before.

"Our readers will remember that the police, while attempting to arrest one Ellwell for the jewel-robbery which occurred in the city some time ago, were compelled to fire on the man in self-defence. He died last night in the arms of a female relative, who had been sent for at his request. He was known by various names – Durocher, Gillet, etc. – and the police have had much trouble with him."

"There!" said the widow.

"Well, what of that?"

"He died in the arms of a female relative."

"Well, were you the relative?"

"Indeed! my fine fellow, be careful! Do you think I would be the female relative of a convict? Do you not know any of these names?" The postmaster felt guilty; he did know one of the names.

"They are common enough," he replied. "The name of my aunt's second husband was Durocher."

"It will not do!" said the widow. "Somebody builds a house, no one knows who; people come and go, no one knows how; and you, a stupid postmaster, shut your eyes and help things along."

Three days after this, Mademoiselle Viau came home. She was no longer the little one in gray; she was the little one in black. She came straight to Monsieur Cuerrier to get her cat. Then she went home. The widow watched her go in. "Now," she said, "we will not see her come out again."

Mademoiselle Viau refused to take any more work. She was sick, she said; she wanted to rest. She rested for two weeks, and Monsieur Cuerrier brought her food ready cooked. Then he stopped; she was better. One evening Madame Laroque peeped in at the side window. She saw the little milliner quite distinctly. She was on her knees, her face was hidden in her arms. The fire was very bright, and the lamp was lighted.

Two days after that the widow said to Cuerrier: "It is very strange there is no smoke. Has Mademoiselle Viau gone away?"

"Yes, she has gone."

"Did you see her go?"

"No."

"It is as I said – no one has seen her go. But wait, she will come back; and no one will see her come."

That was three years ago, and she has not come back. All the white curtains are pulled down. Between the one that covers the front window and the sash stands the pot in which grew the geranium. It only had one blossom all the time it was alive, and it is dead now and looks like a dry stick. No one knows what will become of the house. Madame Laroque thinks that Monsieur Cuerrier knows. She expects, some morning, to look across and see the little milliner cast down crumbs for the birds. In the meantime, in every corner of the house the spiders are weaving webs, and an enterprising caterpillar has blocked up the key-hole with his cocoon.

The Desjardins

JUST AT THE foot of the hill, where the bridge crossed the Blanche, stood one of the oldest houses in Viger. It was built of massive timbers. The roof curved and projected beyond the eaves, forming the top of a narrow veranda. The whole house was painted a dazzling white except the window-frames, which were green. There was a low stone fence between the road and the garden, where a few simple flowers grew. Beyond the fence was a row of Lombardy poplars, some of which had commenced to die out. On the opposite side of the road was a marshy field, where by day the marsh marigolds shone, and by night, the fire-flies. There were places in this field where you could thrust down a long pole and not touch bottom. In the fall a few musk-rats built a house there, in remembrance of the time when it was a favorite wintering-ground. In the spring the Blanche came up and flowed over it. Beyond that again the hill curved round, with a scarped, yellowish slope.

In this house lived Adèle Desjardin with her two brothers, Charles and Philippe. Their father was dead, and when he died there was hardly a person in the whole parish who was sorry. They could remember him as a tall, dark, forbidding-looking man, with long arms out of all proportion to his body. He had inherited his fine farm from his father, and had added to and improved it. He had always been prosperous, and was considered the wealthiest man in the parish. He was inhospitable, and became more taciturn and morose after his wife died. His pride was excessive and kept him from associating with his neighbors, although he was in no way above them. Very little was known about his manner of life, and there was a mystery about his father's death. For some time the old man had not been seen about the place, when one day he came from the city, dead, and in his coffin, which was thought strange. This gave rise to all sorts of rumor and gossip; but the generally accredited story was, that there was insanity in the family and that he had died crazy.

However cold Isidore Desjardin was to his neighbors, no one could have charged him with being unkind or harsh with his children, and as they grew up he gave them all the advantages which it was possible for them to have. Adèle went for a year to the Convent of the Sacre Coeur in the city, and could play tunes on the piano when she came back; so that she had to have a piano of her own, which was the first one ever heard in Viger. She was a slight, angular girl, with a dark, thin face and black hair and eyes. She looked like her father, and took after him in many ways. Charles, the elder son, was like his grandfather, tall and muscular, with a fine head and a handsome face. He was studious and read a great deal, and was always talking to the curé about studying the law. Philippe did not care about books; his father could never keep him at school. He was short and thick-set and had merry eyes, set deep in his head. "Some one must learn to look after things," he said, and when his father died he took sole charge of everything.

If the Desjardins were unsociable with others, they were happy among themselves. Almost every evening during the winter, when the work was done, they would light up the front room with candles, and Adèle would play on the piano and sing. Charles would pace to and fro behind her, and Philippe would thrust his feet far under the stove, that projected from the next room through the partition, and fall fast asleep. Her songs were mostly old French songs, and she could sing "Partant pour la Syrie" and "La Marseillaise." This last was a favorite with Charles; he could not sing himself, but he accompanied the music by making wild movements with his arms, tramping heavily up and down before the piano, and shouting out so loudly as to wake Philippe, "Aux armes, citoyens!" On fine summer evenings Philippe and Adèle would walk up and down the road, watching the marsh fire-flies, and pausing on the bridge to hear the fish jump in the pool, and the deep, vibrant croak of the distant frogs. It was not always Philippe who walked there with Adèle; he some-times sat on the veranda and watched her walk with some one else. He would have waking dreams, as he smoked, that the two figures moving before him were himself and some one into whose eyes he was looking.

At last it came to be reality for him, and then he could not sit quietly and watch the lovers; he would let his pipe go out, and stride impatiently up and down the veranda. And on Sunday afternoons he would harness his horse, dress himself carefully, and drive off with short laughs, and twinklings of the eyes, and wavings of the hands. They were evidently plan-ning the future, and it seemed a distance of vague happiness.

Charles kept on his wonted way; if they talked in the parlor, they could hear him stirring upstairs; if they strolled in the road, they could see his light in the window. Philippe humored his studious habits; he only worked in the morn-ings; in the afternoons he read, history principally. His favorite study was the "Life of Napoleon Buonaparte," which seemed to absorb him completely. He was growing more retired and preoccupied every day, – lost in deep reveries, swallowed of ambitious dreams.

It had been a somewhat longer day than usual in the harvest-field, and it was late when the last meal was ready. Philippe, as he called Charles, from the foot of the stair, could hear him walking up and down, seemingly reading out loud, and when he received no response to his demand he went up the stairs. Pushing open the door, he saw his brother striding up and down the room, with his hands clasped behind him and his head bent, muttering to himself.

"Charles!" He seemed to collect himself, and looked up. "Come down to supper!" They went downstairs together. Adèle and Philippe kept up a conversation throughout the meal, but Charles hardly spoke. Suddenly he pushed his plate away and stood upright, to his full height; a look of calm, severe dignity came over his face.

"I!" said he; "I am the Great Napoleon!"

"Charles!" cried Adèle, "what is the matter?"

"The prosperity of the nation depends upon the execution of my plans. Go!" said he, dismissing some imaginary person with an imperious gesture.

They sat as if stunned, and between them stood this majestic figure with outstretched hand. Then Charles turned away and commenced to pace the room.

"It has come!" sobbed Adèle, as she sank on her knees beside the table.

"There is only one thing to do," said Philippe, after some hours of silence. "It is hard; but there is only one thing to do." The room was perfectly dark; he stood in the window, where he had seen the light die out of the sky, and now in the marshy field he saw the fire-flies gleam. He knew that Adèle was in the dark somewhere beside him, for he could hear her breathe. "We must cut ourselves off; we must be the last of our race." In those words, which in after years were often on his lips, he seemed to find some comfort, and he continued to repeat them to himself.

Charles lay in bed in a sort of stupor for three days. On Sunday morning he rose. The church bells were ringing. He met Philippe in the hall.

"Is this Sunday?" he asked.

"Yes."

"Come here!" They went into the front room.

"This is Sunday, you say. The last thing I remember was you telling me to go in – that was Wednesday. What has happened?" Philippe dropped his head in his hands.

"Tell me, Philippe, what has happened?"

"I cannot."

"I must know, Philippe; where have I been?"

"On Wednesday night," said he, as if the words were choking him, "you said, 'I am the Great Napoleon!' Then you said something about the nation, and you have not spoken since."

Charles dropped on his knees beside the table against which Philippe was leaning. He hid his face in his arms. Philippe, reaching across, thrust his fingers into his brother's brown hair. The warm grasp came as an answer to all Charles's unasked questions; he knew that, whatever might happen, his brother would guard him.

For a month or two he lay wavering between two worlds; but when he saw the first snow, and lost sight of the brown earth, he at once commenced to order supplies, to write despatches, and to make preparations for the gigantic expedition which was to end in the overthrow of the Emperor of all the Russias. And the snow continues to bring him this activity; during the summer he is engaged, with no very definite operations, in the field, but when winter comes he always prepares for the invasion of Russia. With the exception of certain days of dejection and trouble, which Adèle calls the Waterloo days, in the summer he is triumphant with perpetual victory. On a little bare hill, about a mile from the house, from which you can get an extensive view of the sloping country, he watches the movements of the enemy. The blasts at the distant quarries sound in his ears like the roar of guns. Beside him the old gray horse, that Philippe has set apart for his service, crops the grass or stands for hours patiently. Down in the shallow valley the Blanche runs, glistening; the mowers sway and bend; on the horizon shafts of smoke rise, little clouds break away from the masses and drop their quiet shadows on the fields. And through his glass Charles watches the moving shadows, the shafts of smoke, and the swaying mowers, watches the distant hills fringed with beech-groves. He despatches his aides-de-camp with important orders, or rides down the slope to oversee the fording of the Blanche. Half-frightened village boys hide in the long grass to hear him go muttering by. In the autumn he comes sadly up out of the valley, leading his horse, the rein through his arm and his hands in his coat-sleeves. The sleet dashes against him, and the wind rushes and screams around him, as he ascends the little knoll. But whatever the weather, Philippe waits in the road for him and helps him dismount. There is something heroic in his short figure.

"Sire, my brother!" he says; – "Sire let us go in!"

"Is the King of Rome better?"

"Yes."

"And the Empress?"

"She is well."

Only once has a gleam of light pierced these mists. It was in the year when, as Adèle said, he had had two Waterloos and had taken to his bed in consequence. One evening Adèle brought him a bowl of gruel. He stared like a child awakened from sleep when she carried in the lamp. She approached the bed, and he started up.

"Adèle!" he said, hoarsely, and pulling her face down, kissed her lips. For a moment she had hope, but with the next week came winter; and he commenced his annual preparations for the invasion of Russia.

The Wooing of Monsieur Cuerrier

IT HAD BEEN one of those days that go astray in the year, and carry the genius of their own month into the alien ground of another. This one had mistaken the last month of spring for the last month of summer, and had lighted a May day with an August sun. The tender foliage of the trees threw almost transparent shadows, and the leaves seemed to burn with a green liquid fire in the windless air. Toward noon the damp fields commenced to exhale a moist haze that spread, gauze-like, across the woods. Growing things seemed to shrink from this heavy burden of sun, and if one could have forgotten that there were yet trilliums in the woods, he might have expected summer sounds on the summer air. After the sun had set the atmosphere hung dense, falling into darkness without a movement, and when night had come the sultry air was broken by flashes of pale light, that played fitfully and without direction. People sat on their door-steps for air, or paced the walks languidly. It was not a usual thing for Monsieur Cuerrier to go out after nightfall; his shop was a general rendezvous, and the news and the gossip of the neighborhood came to him without his search. But something had been troubling him all day, and at last, when his evening mail was closed, he put on his boots and went out. He sauntered down the street in his shirt sleeves, with his fingers in his vest pockets. His face did not lose its gravity until he had seated himself opposite his friend Alexis Girouard, and put a pipe between his teeth. Then he looked over the candle which stood between them, and something gleamed in his eye; he nursed his elbow and surveyed his friend. Alexis Girouard was a small man, with brown side-whiskers; his face was so round, and the movements of his person so rapid, that he looked like a squirrel whose cheeks are distended with nuts. By occupation he was a buyer of butter and eggs, and went about the country in a calash, driving his bargains. This shrewd fellow, whom no one could get the better of at trade, was ruled by his maiden sister with a rod of iron. He even enjoyed the friendship of Cuerrier by sufferance; their interviews were carried on almost clandestinely, with the figure of the terrible Diana always imminent.

When a sufficient cloud of smoke was spread around the room, Cuerrier asked, "Where is she?" Alexis darted a glance in the direction of the village, removing his pipe and pointing to the same quarter; then he heaved a relieved sigh, and commenced smoking again.

"So you are sure she's out?" said Cuerrier.

Alexis looked uneasy. "No," he answered, "I can't be sure she's out."

Cuerrier burst into a hearty laugh. Alexis stepped to the door and listened; when he came back and sat down, Cuerrier said, without looking at him, "Look here, Alexis, I'm going to get married."

His companion started so that he knocked some of the ashes from his pipe, then with a nervous jump he snatched the candle and went into the kitchen. Cuerrier, left in the dark, shook with silent laughter. Alexis came back after making sure that Diana was not there, and before seating himself he held the candle close to his friend's face and surveyed him shrewdly.

"So, are you not mad?"

"No, I'm not mad."

Alexis sat down, very much troubled in mind. "You see I'm not young, and the mother is getting old – see? Now, last week she fell down into the kitchen."

"Well, your getting married won't prevent her falling into the kitchen."

"It is not that so much, Alexis, my good friend, but if you had no one to look after things –" here Alexis winced – "you would perhaps think of it too."

"But you are old – how old?"

Cuerrier took his pipe from his mouth and traced in the air what to Alexis's eyes looked like the figure fifty. Cuerrier offered him the candle. "There is not a gray hair in my head." Girouard took the light and glanced down on his friend's shock of brown hair so finely disordered. He sat down satisfied.

"To whom now – tell me what charming girl is to be the postmistress of Viger; is it the Madame Laroque?"

Cuerrier broke again into one of his valiant laughs.

"Guess again," he cried, "you are near it. You'll burn yourself next time."

"Not the second cousin – not possible – not Césarine Angers?"

Cuerrier, grown more sober, had made various signs of acquiescence.

"And what will your friend the widow say?"

"See here, Alexis, she's –" he was going to say something violent – "she's one of the troubles."

"Bah! Who's afraid of her! If you had Diana to deal with, now."

"Well, Alexis, my good friend, that is it. Could you not drop a little hint to the widow some time? Something like this —" he was silent.

"Something like a dumb man, eh?"

"Paufh! I have no way with the women, you will make a little hint to the widow."

Just then there was a sound of footsteps on the walk. Alexis promptly blew out the candle, grasped his friend by the arm, and hurried him through the dark to the door. There he thrust his hat into his hand, and saying in his ear, "Good-night – good luck," bolted the door after him.

The night had changed its mood. A gentle breeze, laden with soft moisture, blew from the dark woods; the mist was piled in a gray mass along the horizon; and in spaces of sky as delicately blue as blanched violets, small stars flashed clearly.

Cuerrier pursed up his lips and whistled the only tune he knew, one from "La Fille de Madame Angot." He was uneasy, too uneasy to follow the intricacies of his tune, and he stopped whistling. He had told his friend that he was going to marry, and had mentioned the lady's name; but what right had he to do that? "Old fool!" he said to himself. He remembered his feuds with his love's guardian, some of them of years' standing; he thought of his age, he ran through the years he might expect to live, and ended by calculating how much he was worth, valuing his three farms in an instant. He felt proud after that, and Césarine Angers did not seem quite so far off. He resolved, just before sleep caught him, to open the campaign at once, with the help of Alexis Girouard; but in the dream that followed he found himself successfully wooing the widow, wooing her with sneers and gibes, and rehearsals of the old quarrels that seemed to draw her smilingly toward him, as if there was some malign influence at work translating his words into irresistible phrases of endearment.

Monsieur Cuerrier commenced to wear a gallant blue waistcoat all dotted with white spots, and a silk necktie with fringed ends. "You see I am in the fashion now," he explained to his friends. Villeblanc, the superannuated hairdresser, eyed him critically and commenced to suspect him. He blew a whistle of gratification when, one evening in mid-June, he saw the shy Cuerrier drop a rose, full blown, at the feet of Césarine Angers. His gratification was not unmixed when he saw Césarine pick it up and carry it away, blushing delicately. Cuerrier tried to whistle "La Fille de Madame Angot," but his heart leaped into his throat, and his lips curled into a nervous smile.

"So – so!" said Villeblanc. "So – so! I think I'll curl my gentleman's wig for him."

He was not unheedful of the beauty of Césarine. He spoke a word of enigmatical warning to the widow. "You had better put off your weeds. Are we not going to have a wedding?"

This seed fell upon ready ground, and bore an unexpected shoot. From that day the widow wore her best cap on week days. Then along came the good friend, Alexis Girouard, with his little hint. "My friend Cuerrier wants to get married; he's as shy as a bird, but don't be hard on him." The plant blossomed at once. The widow shook her finger at her image in the glass, took on all the colors of the rainbow, and dusted off a guitar of her youth.

Cuerrier came in the evenings and sat awhile with the widow, and that discreet second cousin, hiding her withered rose. Sometimes also with a stunted farmer from near Viger, who wore shoe-packs and smelt of native tobacco and oiled leather. This farmer was designed by the widow for that rebel Césarine, who still resisted behind her barricade, now strengthened by secret supplies of roses from an official of the government itself.

"But it is high time to speak," thought Cuerrier, and one night, when there was not a hint of native tobacco in the air, he said:

"Madame Laroque, I am thinking now of what I would like to happen to me before I grow an old man, and I think to be married would be a good thing. If you make no objection, I would marry the beautiful Césarine here."

The widow gathered her bitter fruit. "Old beast!" she cried, stamping on the guitar; "old enough to be her great-grandfather!"

She drove the bewildered postmaster out of the house, and locked Césarine into her room. She let her come down to work, but watched her like a cat. Forty times a day she cried out, "The old scoundrel!" and sometimes she would break a silence with a laugh of high mockery, that ended with the phrase, "The idea!" that was like the knot to a whip-lash. She even derided Cuerrier from her chamber window if he dared to walk the street. The postmaster bore it; he pursed up his lips to whistle, and said, "Wait." He also went to see his friend Alexis. "I have a plan, Alexis," he said, "if Diana were only out of the road." But Diana was in the road, she was in league with the widow. "Fancy!" she cried, fiercely, "what is to become of us when old men behave so. Why, the next thing I know, Alexis – *Alexis* will want to get married."

Whatever Cuerrier's plan was, he got no chance to impart it. Diana was always in the road, and reported everything to the widow; she, in turn, watched Césarine. But one night, when Alexis was supposed to be away, he appeared suddenly in Cuerrier's presence. He had come back unexpectedly, and had not gone home first. The plan was imparted to him. "But to bring the calash out of the yard at half-past twelve at night without Diana hearing, never – never – she has ears like a watchdog." But he pledged himself to try. The widow saw him depart, and she and Diana expected a *coup-d'état*. Madame Laroque turned the key on Césarine, and fed her on bread and water; Diana locked her brother's door every night, when she knew he was in bed, much to Alexis's perplexity.

The lane that separated the widow's house from Cuerrier's was just nine feet wide. The postmaster had reason to know that; Madame Laroque had fought him for years, saying that he had built on her land. At last they had got a surveyor from the city, who measured it with his chain. The widow flew at him. He shrugged his shoulders. "The Almighty made this nine feet," he said, "you cannot turn the world upside down."

"Nine feet," said Cuerrier to himself, "nine feet, and two are eleven." With that length in his head he walked over to the carpenter's. That evening he contemplated a two-inch plank eleven feet long in his kitchen. The same evening Alexis was deep in dissimulation. He was holding up an image of garrulous innocence to Diana, who glared at it suspiciously.

The postmaster bored a small hole through the plank about two inches from one end, through this he ran the end of a long rope and knotted it firmly. Then he carried the plank upstairs into a small room over the store. Opposite the window of this room there was a window in Madame Laroque's house.

"Good-night, sweet dreams," cried Alexis to Diana, as, cold with excitement, he staggered upstairs. He made all the movements of undressing but he did not undress; then he gradually quieted down and sat shivering near the window. In a short time Diana crept up and locked his door. It took him an hour to gain courage enough to throw his boots out of the window; he followed them, slipping down the post of the veranda. He crept cautiously into the stable; his horse was ready harnessed and he led her out, quaking lest she should whinny. The calash was farther back in the yard than usual; to drive out he would have to pass Diana's window. Just as he took the reins in his hand the horse gave a loud, fretful neigh; he struck her with the whip, but she would not stir. He struck her again, and, as she bounded past the window it was raised, and something white appeared. Alexis, glancing over his shoulder, gave a hoarse shout, to relieve his excitement; he had seen the head of the chaste Diana.

Cuerrier let down the top window-sash about two inches, then he raised the lower sash almost to its full height, and passed the end of the rope from the outside through the upper aperture into the room, and tied it to a nail. Then he pushed the plank out of the window, and let it drop until it swung by the rope; then he lifted it up hand over hand till the end rested on the sill. Adjusting it so as to leave a good four inches to rest on the opposite ledge, he lowered away his rope until the end of the plank reached the opposite side, and there was a strong bridge from Madame Laroque's house to his own. He took a stout pole and tapped gently on the window. Césarine was stretched on her bed, sleeping lightly. The tapping woke her; she rose on her elbow; the sound came again; she went to the window and raised a corner of the curtain. Cuerrier flashed his lantern across the glass. Césarine put up the window quietly. She heard Cuerrier calling her assuringly. She crept out on the plank, and put the window down. Then she stood up, and, aided by the stout pole, which the postmaster held firmly, she was soon across the abyss. The plank was pulled in, the window shut down, and all trace of the exploit had vanished.

At sunrise, pausing after the ascent of a hill, they looked back, and Césarine thought she saw, like a little silver point in the rosy light, the steeple of the far St. Joseph's, and below them, from a hollow filled with mist, concealing the houses, rose the tower and dome of the parish church of St. Valérie.

A week after, when the farmer from near Viger came into the post-office for his mail, bearing the familiar odor of native tobacco, the new postmistress of Viger, setting the tips of her fingers on the counter, and leaning on her pretty wrists until four dimples appeared on the back of each of her hands, said, "I have nothing for you."

The rage of Madame Laroque was less than her curiosity to know how Césarine had effected her escape. She made friends with her, and wore a cheerful face, but Césarine was silent. "Tell her 'birds fly,'" said Cuerrier. Exasperated, at last, the widow commenced a petty revenge. She cooked a favorite dinner of Cuerrier's, and left her kitchen windows open to fill his house with the odor. But, early that morning, the postmaster had gone off to St. Valérie to draw up a lease, and had taken his wife with him. About noon he had stopped to water his horse, and had climbed out of his calash to pluck some asters; Césarine decked her hat with them, and sang a light song – she had learned the air from "La Fille de Madame Angot."

Sedan

ONE OF THE pleasantest streets in Viger was that which led from the thoroughfare of the village to the common. It was a little street with little houses, but it looked as if only happy people lived there. The enormous old willows which shaded it through its whole length made a perpetual shimmer of shadow and sun, and towered so above the low cottages that they seemed to have crept under the guardian trees to rest and doze a while. There was something idyllic about this contented spot; it seemed to be removed from the rest of the village, to be on the boundaries of Arcadia, the first inlet to its pleasant, dreamy fields. In the spring the boys made a veritable Arcadia of it, coming there in bands, cutting the willows for whistles, and entering into a blithe contest for supremacy in making them, accompanying their labors by a perpetual sounding of their pleasant pipes, as if a colony of uncommon birds had taken up their homes in the trees. Even in the winter there was something pleasant about it; the immense boles of the willows, presiding over the collection of houses, seemed to protect them, and the sunshine had always a suggestion of warmth as it dwelt in the long branches. It was on this street, just a little distance from the corner, that Paul Arbique kept his inn, which was famous in its way. He called it The Turenne, after the renowned commander of that name, for they had the same birthplace, and Arbique himself had been a soldier, as his medals would testify. The location was favorable for such a house as Arbique was prepared to keep, and in choosing it he appealed to a crotchet in man which makes it pleasanter for him to go around the corner for anything he may require. A pleasant place it was, particularly in summer. The very exterior had an air about it, the green blinds and the green slatted door, and the shadows from the willow-leaves playing over the legend "Fresh Buttermilk," a sign dear to the lover of simple pleasures.

From all the appearances one would have supposed that The Turenne was a complete success, and every one thought Arbique was romancing when he said he was just getting along, and that was all. But so far as he knew he spoke the truth, for his wife managed everything, including himself. There was only one thing she could not do; she could not make him stop drinking brandy.

The Arbiques considered themselves very much superior to the village people, because they had come from old France. "I am a Frenchman," Paul would say, when he had had too much brandy; but no one would take offence at him, he was too good a fellow. When he had had a modicum of his favorite liquor he talked of his birthplace, Sedan, the dearest spot on earth to him, and his Crimean experiences; and when he had reached a stage beyond that he talked of his wife. It was a pathetic sight to see him at such times, as he leaned close to his auditor, and explained to him how superior a woman Felice was, and what a cruel, inexplicable mistake she had made in marrying him, and how all his efforts to make her happy had failed, not through any fault of her own, but because it was impossible that he could ever make her happy; thus taking all the blame of their domestic infelicity upon his own shoulders, with the simple idea that it must be his own fault when no fault of any kind could possibly rest with Felice.

He was a tall chivalrous-looking fellow, with a military air, and despite his fifty years and the extent of his potations there was yet a brave flourish in his manner. He was seen at his best on Sunday, when, clothed in a complete suit of black, with a single carnation in his buttonhole, and with an irreproachable silk hat, he promenaded with Madame Arbique on his arm. Madame on such occasions was as fine as her lord, and held her silk gown far above the defilement of the street, in order to show her embroidered petticoat and a pair of pretty feet. But no matter how finely she was dressed she always wore an expression of discontent. She had the instincts of a miser, but she also had enough good sense not to let them interfere with the sources of profit, and so, although she was as keen to save a cent as any one could have been, The Turenne showed no sign of it. The provision for the entertainment of guests was ample and sufficient. Felice had always had her own way, and owing to Paul's incapacity, which had overtaken him gradually, the affairs of the house had been left in her hands.

They had only had one child, who had died when she was a baby, and this want of children was a great trial to Paul. They had attempted to fill her place by adopting a little girl, but the experiment had not been a success, and she grew to be something between a servant and a poor relation working for her board. This was owing to no fault of Paul's, who would have prevented it if he could, but his wife had taken a dislike to the child, and she simply neglected her. Latulipe, for in the family she was called by no other name, was a strange girl. She had been frightened and subdued by Madame Arbique, and at times she would scarcely speak a word, and then again she would talk boldly and defiantly, as if she were protesting, no matter how insignificant her remarks might be. Her personal appearance was as odd as her manner; she had an abundance of hair, of a light, pleasant shade of red, her complexion was a clear white, her lips were intensely crimson, her dark eyes were small but quick, and very clear. Her manner was shy, and rather awkward. Her one claim to distinction was that she had some influence over Arbique, whom she could now and then prevent drinking. He was sorry for her, and ashamed of the position she occupied in the house, which was so different from what he had intended.

When the Franco-Prussian war broke out, and for months before, The Turenne was the rendezvous for those of the villagers who had any desire to discuss the situation. Arbique was the oracle of this group, and night after night he held forth on the political situation, on the art of war, and his personal experiences in the army. There was only one habitué of The Turenne who was silent on these occasions, that was Hans Blumenthal, the German watchmaker. He had had his corner in the barroom ever since he had come to Viger, and was one of Arbique's best customers. But when the war excitement broke out Arbique expected to see no more of him; the warmth of the discussions and the violence of the treatment his nation received nightly would have been expected to drive him away. But instead, he returned again and again to his place at the little table by the window, peering through his glasses with his imperturbable, self-absorbed expression, not seeming to heed the wordy storms that beset his ears.

Arbique, when hostilities had actually broken out, pasted a map of the seat of war upon the wall; above this he placed a colored picture of a French chasseur, and scrawled below it the words "*A Berlin!*" Even this did not disturb the German. He took advantage of the map, and as Arbique had set pins, to which were attached red and blue pieces of wool, to show the positions of the armies, he even studied the locations and movements with interest. He read his paper, gave his orders, paid his score, came and went as he had always done. This made Paul very angry, and he would have turned him out of the house if he had not remembered that he was his guest, and his sense of honor would not permit it. He was drinking very heavily and wanted to fight some one, but every one agreed with him except the German, and he kept silence. He had serious thoughts of challenging him to a duel, if the opportunity offered.

Latulipe was the only one who stood up for Hans. She had been accustomed to wait on the guests sometimes, when Arbique was incapacitated, and his gentle manner had won her regard. One day she turned on Paul, who was abusing Hans behind his back, and gave him a piece of her mind. She was so sudden and sharp with it that she sobered him a little, and in thinking it over he came to the conclusion that if he could help it she would see the German no more. Hans noticed her absence, and said to Paul one night when he was ordering his beer: "Where is Mademoiselle Latulipe?" By the way he said it, in his odd French, any one could have told what he thought of Latulipe. "Mademoiselle Latulipe," said Arbique, with a dramatic flourish, "is my daughter." So Hans saw her no more in the evening.

He had other trials besides this. Once in a while the lads in the street hooted after him, and this sort of attention became more frequent. One evening, after the news of Woerth had been received, some one threw a stone through the window of his shop. That very night he stood before the map with his hands behind him, peering into it; as he altered the pins, which Arbique had now lost all interest in, he heard some one mutter "*Scélérat!*" He thought it must be intended for him, but he drank his beer quietly and went home rather early. After he had gone some of his enemies, becoming valiant with liquor, made a compact to go out when it was late enough, break into his house, and give him a sound beating. But Latulipe overheard their plan from the stairway, and as soon as she could get away without being noticed, she ran over to the watchmaker's shop. It was quite late and there was not a soul on the street. She was wondering how she could warn him, but when she reached the door she noticed a ladder which led to a scaffold running along below the windows of the second story, where some workmen had been making repairs. There was a light burning in one of the second story windows, and without waiting to reflect Latulipe ran up the ladder and tapped at the window. Hans opened it, and said something in German when he saw who it was. Latulipe did not wait for salutations, but told him exactly what he might expect. When that was over she tried to escape as she had come, but the darkness below frightened her, and she could not go down the ladder. Hans tried to coax her to come in at the window and go out by the street door, but she would not hear to that; she leaned against the house, shrinking away from the edge. So Hans got out upon the scaffolding. "Mademoiselle Latulipe," he said, in his rough French, "you need not be alarmed at me; I have only a good heart toward you." He held out his hand, but Latulipe knew by the sound of his voice that he was going to make love to her, and before he could say another word she was at the bottom of the ladder. When the bravos came to give Hans his beating he confronted them with a lamp in one hand and a pistol in the other, and they fell over one another in their haste to retreat.

During the whole of the month of August Arbique had been wild with excitement; he could think of nothing but the war, and would talk of nothing else. At first he would not believe in any reverse to the French arms; it was impossible – lies, lies, everything was lies. His cry was "*A Berlin!*" But although he could manage to deceive himself by this false enthusiasm, sometimes the truth would stab straight to his heart like a knife, and he would tremble as if he had the ague, for the honor of his country was the thing dearest to him in all the world. If he could only have died for her! But there, day after day, he saw the pins on the map, moved by that cold German, close around Metz. He could no longer cry "*A*

Berlin;" the French army was facing Paris, with Berlin at its back. He drank fiercely now, and even Latulipe could do nothing with him. Madame Arbique knew that he would drink himself to death, as his father had done. He would sit and mutter by the hour, thinking all the time of what revenge he could have on Blumenthal, who had become to his eyes the incarnation of hated Prussia. But so long as Hans came to the house quietly to sit at his table and drink his beer Arbique would not say an uncivil word to him.

On the evening of the 28th of August there was an unusual crowd at The Turenne, and a group had surrounded the map gesticulating and discussing. Hans had finished reading his paper, and went toward them. They parted when they saw him coming, and he stood peering down at the map through his glasses. Arbique had not been seen all evening, but he appeared suddenly, looking haggard and shattered, and caught sight of his friends grouped round the German. He went slowly toward them, and as he approached he heard Hans say: "There, there they must fight," and saw him put his finger on the map between Mézières and Carignan, almost over Sedan.

Paul had been in bed all day, and had not had anything to drink, and when he saw the German with his finger on Sedan he could not stand it any longer. He broke out: "No, not there – here," his voice trembling with rage. "Here they will fight – you for your abominable Prussia, I for my beautiful France." He fell into a dramatic attitude. Drawing two pistols from his pocket, he presented one to his nearest friend to hand to Blumenthal. The man held the pistol for a moment, but Hans never moved. Madame Arbique, seeing the commotion, and catching sight of the weapons, screamed as loud as she could, and Latulipe, running in, threw herself upon Arbique. He turned deadly pale and had to use the girl's strength to keep from falling. Hans went away quietly, and sat down near the window. Arbique was fluttering like a leaf in the wind, and

Latulipe and Felice half carried him upstairs. The men left in the room shook their heads.

The next evening Hans was walking in the starlight, under the willows. With his dim vision he saw some one leaning against one of the trees, but when he passed again he knew it was Latulipe. He stopped and spoke to her. When she spoke she did not answer his question. "Oh," she said, "he will never get better, never." "Yes," said Hans, "he will be better." "No," said Latulipe, "I know by the way he looks, and he says now that France is beaten and crushed he does not want to live." "Brave soul!" said Hans. "And when he goes," said Latulipe, "what is to become of me?" He laid his hand upon her arm, and when she did not resist, he took her hand in both his own. She was giving herself to the enemy. A cloud above had taken the starlight, and in the willows a little rain fell with a timorous sound. Latulipe was crying softly on Hans's shoulder.

It was September, and around Viger the harvest was nearly finished. The days were clear as glass; already the maples were stroked with fire, with the lustre of wine and gold; early risers felt the keener air; the sunsets reddened the mists which lay light as lawn on the low fields. But Paul Arbique thought and spoke of Sedan alone, the place where he was born, of the Meuse, the bridges, of his father's farm, just without the walls of the city, and of his boyhood, and the friends of his youth. His thoughts were hardly of the war, or of the terror of the downfall which had a little while before so haunted him.

It was the evening of the day upon which the news of the battle had come. They had resolved not to tell him, but there was something in Latulipe's manner which disturbed him. Waking from a light doze, he said: "That Prussian spy, what did he say? – they must fight there – between Mézières and Carignan? I have been at Carignan – and he had his hound's paw on Sedan." He was quiet for a while; then he said, dreamily: "They – have – fought." Latulipe, who was watching with him, wept. In the night his lips moved again. "France," he murmured, "France will rise – again." It was toward the morning of the next day when his true heart failed. Latulipe had just opened the blinds. A pale light came through the willows. When she bent over him she caught his last word. "Sedan." He sighed. "Sedan."

No. 68 Rue Alfred de Musset

IT WAS AN evening early in May. The maples were covered with their little seed-pods, like the crescents of the Moslem hosts they hung redly in the evening air. The new leaf-tips of the poplars shone out like silver blooms. The mountain-ash-trees stood with their virginal branches outlined against the filmy rose and gray of the evening sky, their slender leaves half open. Everything swam in the hazy light; the air was full of gold motes; in the sky lay a few strands of cloud, touched with almost imperceptible rose. At the upper window of a house in De Musset Street, Maurice Ruelle looked down upon the trees covered with the misty light. His window was high above everything, and the house itself stood alone on the brow of a little cliff that commanded miles of broken country. Maurice was propped up at the window, and had a shawl thrown about his shoulders. The room was close; a little wood-fire was dying away in the open stove.

"Maurice, Maurice, I'm sick of life. I will be an adventuress."

Maurice turned his head to look at the speaker. She was seated on the floor, leaning on her slanted arm, which was thrown behind her to support her weight.

"Well, my dear sister, you are ambitious –"

"Don't be bitter, Maurice."

"I'm not bitter; I know you are ambitious; I am proud of you, you know. I don't see why you have to nurse me; fate is cruel to you."

"Oh, but I don't nurse you, you know that; what's my nursing good for? I only wish we had money enough to send you away for these terrible winters, or give you a room in some fine hospital."

Maurice watched the birds dropping through the glow. A little maid brought in candles. Eloise began to walk up and down the room restlessly.

"Ah, well, we haven't the money," Maurice sighed.

"Money – money – it's not altogether a matter of money; to me it's a matter of life."

"Well, to me it's hardly a matter of money or of life."

"Maurice, you must not think of that; I forbid it. I must do something. I feel that I can succeed. Look at me, Maurice – tell me now –"

She stood with her head thrown back, and poised lightly, and with a little frown on her face.

"Superb!" said her brother.

"I know I'll do something desperate," she said. "I must live; I was made to."

"Yes, my dear, that is the difference between us."

"Maurice, how dare you; I forbid it; I have decided. You will go south, and I will begin to live. I am going to stop wishing."

"Well, I have long ago ceased to wish; wishing was the only passion I ever had; I have given it up. But I have not wished for money; sometimes I have wished for health –"

He did not finish his sentence; he only thought of what he had longed for more than anything else, the love of his beautiful, impulsive sister. Eloise was dusting her geranium leaves. Maurice looked from his window into the tree on which the leaves were not yet thick enough to hide the old nests.

A short time after this a rather curious advertisement appeared in one of the city papers. It read: "Very handsome old oak furniture. Secretaire with small drawers. A dower chest and a little table. Each article richly carved. For particulars call at No. 68 Rue Alfred de Musset, Viger."

Eloise read this advertisement to her brother.

"What does this mean?" he asked. "We have no such furniture, but it is our number true enough. Is this the commencement?"

"Yes, my dear, that is what it is."

The next day callers in response to this advertisement began to arrive. Eloise answered the bell herself. The first was a rather shabby old man who wore a tall hat and green glasses. He produced a crumpled clipping from the paper, and, smoothing it out, handed it to Eloise.

"I have come to buy this second-hand furniture," he explained, holding his hat by the brim. Eloise looked at the advertisement as if she had never seen it before.

"There must be some mistake," she said. "I have no such furniture."

"I have not mistaken the number – No. 68 Rue Alfred de Musset."

"Yes, but the printer must have made a mistake; this is not the place."

Many times that day she had to give unpromising looking people the same answer. Every one of them accepted the situation cheerfully; certainly it must have been a mistake. Three letters came also with inquiries about the furniture. One of these Eloise was tempted to answer; but she resolved to wait a day or two. The next day no one came at all; but on the next, about four o'clock in the afternoon, a young man drove up in a dog-cart. He left his horse, and walked rapidly through the little garden to the house. He was a handsome vigorous-looking youth. He rang somewhat violently; and Eloise answered the summons. She opened the door a foot, and the caller could only see a bit of her white dress.

"I have called to see the furniture you have advertised," he said.

The door opened slowly, and, taking this as an invitation to enter, he stepped into the hall. He could not tell why, but he expected to see an old woman behind the door; instead he saw a very graceful girl holding the door-knob between her fingers. Without a word she preceded him with an air of shyness, and led the way into the front room. He glanced about for the furniture; it was evidently not there. She asked him to be seated.

"My father wanted me to come out and look at the things you advertised," he said.

"You are very good, Monsieur."

"Not at all; my father picks up these things, for the house, when they are really valuable."

"These are very valuable."

She still wore an air of shyness, and looked abstractedly from the window into a lilac-bush; she seemed nervous and apprehensive.

"Could you let me see them?"

There was a noise upstairs. Eloise half started from her chair.

"I beg of you not to speak so loudly."

He relapsed into a whisper.

"I beg pardon, I was not conscious of speaking too loudly."

"It is not that, but – I cannot explain." She ended abruptly. "You see," she said, hesitatingly, "I wish you had come yesterday."

"Have you promised them to some one else?"

"No, not at all; but yesterday it might have been possible, to-day it is impossible to show it to you."

"When can I see it?"

"I am unfortunate – I cannot say when. It is my brother's – but it must be sold."

An expression of slight distress crossed her face.

"Does he not want it sold?"

"Monsieur, I beg of you not to question me; I am in great perplexity." She continued, after a moment's pause, "You have rarely seen things so exquisite; the secretaire has a secret cabinet, the chest is carved with a scene of nymphs in a wood; the table is a beautiful little table." She figured these articles in the air with an imaginative wave of her hand. The young man began to regard her with some interest; he remarked to himself that she was a lovely girl.

"I'm sorry my call is inopportune, I will come again." He left his card on the table.

"Perhaps when you come again it will be more convenient," she said, following him at some distance to the door. He opened it himself, and went down the steps; as he looked back it was slowly shutting, and he caught a glimpse of her delicate white dress as it closed. Eloise took up the card. The name was Pierre Pechito. She knew the name; it was borne by one of the richest of the city merchants. She took the card up to Maurice. He held it in his emaciated fingers.

"Is this the end of Chapter One?" he asked. "Well, he may never come back; and what will you do with him if he does come back?"

"Oh, he will come; as for the rest, we must succeed. But there is one thing, Maurice, you must be the invisible ogre; you must rage about here as wildly as you can, while I am working out our destiny downstairs."

"My destiny?" he asked, with a falling touch of sadness in his accent.

A few days after this Pierre returned. "May I come in?" he asked, as Eloise held the door open hesitatingly.

"If you wish, Monsieur." They sat a moment silently in the parlor.

"Monsieur," said Eloise, commencing hurriedly but determinedly, "in this life everything is uncertain; so much depends upon mere circumstances, which are too obscure for us to control. I am willing to show you the furniture, but how much depends upon that!" She rose with the air of a heroine, and led the way to the foot of the stairs. Pierre followed. She had ascended three steps, and he had his hand on the newel post, when there was a crash in the room above. Eloise turned suddenly and leaned against the banister, glancing up the stairs, and extending her hand to keep Pierre back. "Monsieur, for the love of heaven do not come on, go back – go back into the room, I beg of you."

"I am leaving you in danger, Mademoiselle."

"I am accustomed to it. I beg of you." She accompanied these words with an imploring gesture. Pierre went into the room, where he paced up and down. The noise increased in violence, and then ceased altogether. Eloise returned to the room; she leaned from the window, breathing convulsively; she plucked one of the half-grown lilac leaves and bit it through and through.

"Yet the furniture must be sold," she said aloud. Pierre took a step toward her.

"Mademoiselle, you are in distress. May I not help you? I am able to. You can command me."

"Alas, Monsieur, you mean I can command your wealth." Pierre was profoundly moved at the sorrow in her girlish voice.

"I mean I would help you; I want to do what I can for you."

"Let us go no farther," she said, with her eyes fixed on the floor. "I must not come into your happy life." There was a trace of bitterness in her tone.

"I have undertaken to buy the furniture," he said, with a smile. "I will not give up so soon."

"Maurice, Maurice, you are a splendid ogre!" said Eloise, throwing open the door.

"It is terribly exhausting," he said, with a faint smile.

When Pierre next came it was raining quietly through a silver haze; the little maid opened the door; a moment later Eloise came into the room. When she spoke her voice sounded restrained; and to Pierre she seemed completely different.

"I have deceived you," she commenced, without prelude, "there is no furniture to sell." To all his questions or remonstrances she gave him this answer, as if she were afraid to trust herself to other words, standing with her eyes cast to the floor, and an expressionless face. But when she seemed the most distant, as if she could not recede further, she burst into tears. Pierre hurried toward her – "Mademoiselle, I cannot address you by name; you cannot deceive me; you are in great distress. I beg you not to think of the furniture; it is not necessary that these things of wood should trouble you further; to-day I did not come to see it, I came to see you."

"Oh, Monsieur," she sobbed, "you must never come here again, never – never!"

"Make no mistake, I will come, at least until I can help you, until I know your story." He gained her hand.

"Monsieur, I cannot accept your assistance; but your kindness demands my story."

She told it. She was a lovely girl, caught in a net of circumstances. She was an orphan. Her parents had left her and her brother a little money – too little to live on – they existed. Her brother was a cripple – how often had she wished she was dead – he was wicked. She hinted at unkindness, at tyranny. It was necessary to sell these heirlooms. (Here Pierre pressed her hand, "You could not deceive me," he said.) But he would not hear of it. Her life was intolerable – but she must live it to the end – to the end. "If I could have deceived you, Monsieur, I would have done so." A smile shimmered through her tears. Pierre pressed her hand; she softly drew it away. Suddenly there was a crash in the room above; a light shower of dry whitewash was thrown down around them; the sound of an inhuman voice came feebly down the stairs. "I must go, do not detain me," she cried, as Pierre tried to intercept her. He endeavored to hold her at the foot of the stairs. "Do not go, I beg of you." She turned sweetly toward him. "I must go; it is my duty; you do yours." The tears were not yet dry on her eyelids. Pierre watched her flutter upstairs like a dove flying into a hawk's nest. His pulses were pounding at his wrists. "I wish I knew what my duty was," he said to himself. As he left the house he glanced up at the window, a handkerchief dropped down; he pressed it to his lips and thrust it into his bosom. When he was out of sight he examined it. It was a dainty thing of the most delicate fabric; in one corner were the words, "Eloise Ruelle."

Eloise found Maurice almost fainting with his exertion. When he recovered, he said –

"Is the game worth the candle?"

"Well, we will see."

"Eloise, you have been crying."

"I cry easily, I do everything easily."

Maurice turned away and gazed from the window. The rain was so fine it seemed to be a rising mist; the trees were hidden, like plants in the bottom of the sea; somewhere the sun was shining, for there was a silver bar in the mist.

Pierre was not slow in coming again; but, instead of seeing Eloise, he had a note thrust into his hand by the little serving-maid. It ran: "I cannot see you. *He* forbids it. Who could have told that our last word was 'good-by.' If I could have spoken again I would have thanked you. How can I ever do so now? Adieu." Reading this on the step, he scrawled hurriedly on a leaf of his note-book: "I would not have you thank me, but I must see you again. Your risk is great, but I will be here to-morrow night; we will have the darkness, and all I ask is ten minutes. Is it too much?"

He gave the note to the maid, who shut the door. The house looked absolutely sphinx-like as he walked away from it.

The next night was moist with a touch of frost. A little smoke from burning leaves hung in the air with a pungent odor. The scent of the lilacs fell with the wind when it moved. Eloise was muffled picturesquely in a cloak. Pierre was holding her hand, which she had not reclaimed. "I have dared everything to come," she said softly.

"You are brave, braver than I was to ask you."

"You know my story. You are the only one."

"That binds us."

"How can I thank you?"

"You must not try, I have done nothing."

Just then a burning brand was hurled from the window; it fell into the lilac-tree where it devoured a cone of blossom and withered the leaves around it. It threw up a little springing flame which danced a light on Eloise, who had cowered into a corner by the steps, with her hand over her eyes. Pierre went to her. "Tell me," he said, "what does this mean?"

"Oh," she moaned, "he suspects we are here; he always has a fire on the hottest nights, and he is throwing the sticks out." This led Pierre to expect another one. He caught her by the arm.

"You must come out of danger," he said, "one might fall on your dress." The brand was glowing in spots. He tore it out of the bush and trampled on it. They went to the other side of the steps. It was the season of quick growth. In one day thousands of violets had lit their little tips of yellow fire in the tangle of the underwood; in one day the tulips were moulded into fragile cups of flame burning steady in the sunlight; in one day the lilacs had burst their little clove-like blooms, and were crowding in the dark-green leaves.

Pierre was saying excitedly: "Listen to me. This thing cannot go further. I love you, I am yours. I must protect you. You cannot deny me." Eloise tried to stop him with an imploring gesture. "No," he cried, "you must hear me! you must be mine! I will take you away from here."

"Oh, do not tempt me!" cried Eloise. "I must stay here. I cannot leave him."

"You must leave him. What hold has he upon you? I will never let you go back to this torment, – never. Eloise," he continued seriously, "sometimes we have to decide in a moment the things of a life-time. This is such a moment. Before I pluck this blossom," he said, leaning down to a dwarf lilac-bush bearing one bloom, "I want you to promise to be my wife." A moment later he had plucked the flower, but had dropped it, and had caught Eloise in his arms. She stifled a cry, and gave herself to him.

"Maurice, Maurice," cried Eloise, "look at me, I am triumphant!" He hardly looked at her; he was cowering over the fire, which had smouldered away, and in which the ashes were fluttering about like moths.

"I have done what you asked, that is all," he said, with an effort.

"But it is everything to me; I will never forget you, Maurice, no matter how powerful I may become."

"Alas! you need not remember me for long. Perhaps I will have what I wanted here, in some other star."

A few evenings later Eloise drew the door after her: "Hush!" she said, "the least noise will disturb him." She hesitated, and left the door ajar.

"Do you regret?" whispered Pierre.

"No, but I am leaving everything."

"Yes, even the old furniture; if it had not been for that I would never have known you," he said.

"Everything – everything," murmured Eloise.

She listened for a moment, and then shut the door softly on the empty house: Maurice had gone to the hospital that afternoon; the little maid had been discharged.

"But," she said, holding Pierre's arm and leaning away

from him with her sweet smile, "I have also gained all –
everything."

The next moment they had gone cautiously away.

This was the beginning of her career.

The Bobolink

IT WAS THE sunniest corner in Viger where old Garnaud had built his cabin, – his cabin, for it could not be called a house. It was only of one story, with a kitchen behind, and a workshop in front, where Etienne Garnaud mended the shoes of Viger. He had lived there by himself ever since he came from St. Valérie; every one knew his story, every one liked him. A merry heart had the old shoemaker; it made a merry heart to see him bending his white head with its beautiful features above his homely work, and to hear his voice in a high cadence of good-humored song. The broad window of his cabin was covered with a shutter hinged at the top, which was propped up by a stick slanted from the window-sill. In the summer the sash was removed, and through the opening came the even sound of the Blanche against the bridge piers, or the scythe-whetting from some hidden meadow. From it there was a view of a little pool of the stream where the perch jumped clear into the sun, and where a birch growing on the bank threw a silver shadow-bridge from side to side. Farther up, too, were the willows that wore the yellow tassels in the spring, and the hollow where burr-marigolds were brown-golden in August. On the hill slope stood a delicate maple that reddened the moment summer had gone, which old Etienne watched with a sigh and a shake of the head.

If the old man was a favorite with the elder people of Viger, he was a yet greater favorite with the children. No small portion of his earnings went toward the purchase of sugar candy for their consumption. On summer afternoons he would lay out a row of sweet lumps on his window-sill and pretend to be absorbed by his work, as the children, with much suppressed laughter, darted around the corner of his cabin, bearing away the spoils. He would pause every now and then to call, "Aha – Aha! Where are all my sweeties? those mice and rats must have been after them again!" and would chuckle to himself to hear the children trying to keep back the laughter, out of sight around the corner. In the winter, when the boys and girls would come in to see him work, he always managed to drop some candy into their pockets, which they would find afterward with less surprise than the old man imagined.

But his great friend was the little blind daughter of his neighbor Moreau. "Here comes my little fairy," he would call out, as he saw her feeling her way down the road with her little cedar wand. "Here comes my little fairy," and he would go out to guide her across the one plank thrown over the ditch in front of his cabin. Then they would sit and chat together, this beautiful old man and the beautiful little girl. She raised her soft brown, sightless eyes to the sound of his voice, and he told her long romances, described the things that lay around them, or strove to answer her questions. This was his hardest task, and he often failed in it; her questions ran beyond his power, and left him mystified.

One spring he bought a bobolink from some boys who had trapped it; and he hung its cage in the sun outside his cabin. There it would sing or be silent for days at a time. Little Blanche would sit outside under the shade of the shutter, leaning half into the room to hear the old man talk, but keeping half in the air to hear the bird sing.

They called him "Jack" by mutual consent, and he

absorbed a great deal of their attention. Blanche had to be present at every cage cleaning. One day she said, "Uncle Garnaud, what is he like?"

"Why, dearie, he's a beauty; he's black all over, except his wings and tail, and they have white on them."

"And what are his wings like?"

"Well, now, that finishes me. I am an old fool, or I could tell you."

"Uncle Garnaud, I never even felt a bird; could I feel Jack?"

"Well, I could catch him; but you mustn't squeeze him."

Jack was caught with a sudden dart of the old man's hand; the little blind girl felt him softly, traced the shape of his outstretched wing, and put him back into the cage with a sigh.

"Tell me, Uncle Garnaud," she asked, "how did they catch him?"

"Well, you see, they put a little cage on a stump in the oatfield, and by-and-by the bird flew over and went in."

"Well, didn't he know they would not let him out if he once went in?"

"Well, you know, he hadn't any old uncle to tell him so."

"Well, but birds must have uncles, if they have fathers just like we have."

Old Etienne puckered up his eyes and put his awl through his hair. The bird ran down a whole cadence, as if he was on the wind over a wheat-field; then he stopped.

"There, Uncle Garnaud, I know he must mean something by that. What did he do all day before he was caught?"

"I don't think he did any work. He just flew about and sang all day, and picked up seeds, and sang, and tried to balance himself on the wheat-ears."

"He sang all day? Well, he doesn't do that now."

The bird seemed to recall a sunny field-corner, for his interlude was as light as thistledown, and after a pause he made two little sounds like the ringing of bells at Titania's girdle.

"Perhaps he doesn't like to be shut up and have nobody but us," she said, after a moment.

"Well," said the old man, hesitatingly, "we might let him go."

"Yes," faltered the child, "we might let him go."

The next time little Blanche was there she said, "And he didn't do anything but that, just sing and fly?"

"No, I think not."

"Well, then, he could fly miles and miles, and never come back, if he didn't want to?"

"Why, yes; he went away every winter, so that the frost wouldn't bite him."

"Oh! Uncle Garnaud, he didn't, did he?"

"Yes, true, he did."

The little girl was silent for a while; when the old man looked at her the tears were in her eyes.

"Why, my pretty, what's the matter?"

"Oh, I was just thinking that why he didn't sing was because he only saw you and me, and the road, and our trees, when he used to have everything."

"Well," said the old man, stopping his work, "he might have everything again, you know."

"Might he?" she asked, doubtfully.

"Why, we might let him fly away."

The bird dropped a clear note or two.

"Oh, Uncle Garnaud, do let him go!"

"Why, beauty, just as you say."

The old man put off his apron and took the cage down.

"Here, little girl, you hold the cage, and we'll go where he can fly free."

Blanche carried the cage and he took her hand. They walked down to the bridge, and set the cage on the rail.

"Now, dearie, open the door," said the old man.

The little child felt for the slide and pushed it back. In a moment the bird rushed out and flew madly off.

"He's gone," she said, "Jack's gone. Where did he go, Uncle?"

"He flew right through that maple-tree, and now he's over the fields, and now he's out of sight."

"And didn't he even once look back?"

"No, never once."

They stood there together for a moment, the old man gazing after the departed bird, the little girl setting her brown, sightless eyes on the invisible distance. Then, taking the empty cage, they went back to the cabin. From that day their friendship was not untinged by regret; some delicate mist of sorrow seemed to have blurred the glass of memory. Though he could not tell why, old Etienne that evening felt anew his loneliness, as he watched a long sunset of red and gold that lingered after the footsteps of the August day, and cast a great color into his silent cabin above the Blanche.

The Tragedy of the Seigniory

THERE WAS A house on the outskirts of Viger called, by courtesy, the Seigniory. Passing down one of the side-streets you caught sight of it, set upon a rise, having nothing to do with the street, or seemingly with any part of the town. Built into the bank, as it was, the front had three stories, while the back had but two. The lower flat, half cellar, half kitchen, was lighted from a broad door and two windows facing the southeast. Entrance to the second floor was had by a flight of steps to a wide gallery running completely across the front of the house. Then, above this second story, there was a sharply-peaked roof, with dormer-windows. The walls of the kitchen story were rough stone, while the upper part had been plastered and overlaid with a buff-colored wash; but time had cracked off the plaster in many places, and showed the solid stones.

With all the ravages of time upon it, and with all its old surroundings gone, it yet had an air of some distinction. With its shoulder to the street, and its independent solidity, it made men remember days gone by, when it was only a farm-house on the Estate of the Rioux family. Yet of that estate this old house, with its surrounding three acres of land, was all that remained; and of the retainers that once held allegiance to this proud name, Louis Bois was the last.

Living alone in the old house, growing old with it, guarding some secret and keeping at a proper distance the inquisitive and loquacious villagers, had given Louis also some distinction. He was reported an old soldier, and bore about the witness of it in a wooden leg. He swore, when angry, in a cavalier fashion, using the heavier English oaths with some freedom. His bravery, having never been put to proof, rested securely upon these foundations. But he had a more definite charm for the villagers; he was supposed to have money of his own, and afforded the charming spectacle of a human being vegetating like a plant, without effort and without trouble. Louis Bois had grown large in his indolence, and towards the end of his career he moved with less frequency and greater difficulty. His face was round and fat; the hair had never grown on it, and the skin was fine and smooth as an orange, without wrinkles, but marked with very decided pores. The expression of amiability that his mouth promised was destroyed by an eye of suspicious restlessness. About fifteen years before the time of his release Louis had been sworn to his post by the last of the Rioux family – Hugo Armand Theophile.

This young man, of high spirit and passionate courage, found himself, at the age of twenty-five, after two years of intermittent study at a Jesuit College, fatherless, and without a sou to call his own. Of the family estate, the farm-house, round which Viger had closed, was all that remained, and from its windows this fiery youth might look across the ten acres that were his, over miles of hill and wood to which his grandfather had been born. This vista tortured him for three days, when he sold seven of his acres, keeping the rest from pride. Then he shook off the dust of Viger, but not before swearing Louis Bois, who was old enough to be his father, and loved him as such, to stay and watch the forlorn hope of the Rioux Estate until he, the last of the line, should return and redeem his ancient heritage. He would be gone ten years, he said; and Louis reflected with pride that his own money would keep him that long, and longer.

At first he kept the whole house open, and entertained some of his friends; but he soon discovered that he lost money by that, and gradually he boarded up the windows and lived in the kitchen and one room of the upper flat.

He was a sensitive being, this, and his master's idea had taken hold upon him. His burly frame contained a faint heart; he had no physical courage; and he was as suspicious as a savage. Moreover, he was superstitious, as superstitious as an old wife, and odd occurrences made him uneasy. If he could have been allowed to doze on his gallery in the sun all his days, and sleep secure of dreams and visitations all his nights, his life might have been bearable. The first three years of his stewardship were comparatively uneventful. He traced his liege's progress through the civilized world by the post-mark on his letters, which sometimes contained a bill of exchange, of which the great and safe bank of Bardé Brothers took charge. As yet his master had not captured a treasure ship; but seven years remained.

At the beginning of his fourth year something happened which disturbed Louis' existence to its centre. An emissary of the devil, in the guise of a surveyor, planted his theodolite, and ran a roadway which took off a corner of his three acres, and for this he received only an arbitrator's allowance. In vain he stumped up and down his gallery, and in vain his English oaths – the roadway went through. To add to his trouble, the letters from the wanderer ceased. Was he dead? Had he for-gotten? No more money was coming in, and Louis had the perpetual sight of the alienated lands before his eyes.

One day, when he was coming home from the bank, his eye caught a poster that made him think; it was an announcement of a famous lottery. Do what he would he could not get it out of his head; and that evening, when he was cooking his supper, he resolved to make money after a fashion of his own.

He saw himself a suddenly rich man, the winner of the seventy-five-thousand-dollar prize. He felt his knee burn under him, and felt also what a dead thing his wooden leg was.

He began to venture small sums in the lottery, hoarding half his monthly allowance until he should have sufficient funds to purchase a ticket. Waiting for the moment when he could buy, and then waiting for the moment when he could receive news of the drawing, lent a feverish interest to his life. But he failed to win. With his failure grew a sort of exasperation – he would win, he said, if he spent every cent he owned. He had moments when he suspected that he was being duped, but he was always reassured upon spelling out the lottery circular, where the drawing by the two orphan children was so touchingly described.

At last, after repeated failures, he drew every cent of his own that he could muster, and bought a whole ticket. He never rested a moment until the returns came. He had days of high spirits, when he touched his gains and saw them heaped before him, and other days of depression when he cursed his ill luck, and saw blanks written everywhere. When he learned the result his last disappointment was his greatest. He had drawn a blank.

He was in a perfect fury of rage, and went off to bed cursing like a sea-pirate. When he took off his wooden leg, he took it by the foot and beat the floor with the knee-end until he got some relief. Could he have captured, he would have murdered the innocent orphan children. He swore never to be tempted again, but the morning when he took that oath, April was bleak on the hills, and a tardy spring circled in cold sunshine, leaving the buds suspended.

When May came, his hope again blossomed. Slowly and certainly his mind approached that money he had in trust for his master, until, one sultry day in June, he saw his way to success, and felt his conscience lulled. That afternoon he dozed on the gallery and dreamed. He felt he was in Heaven, and the heaven of his dreams was a large Cathedral whose nave he had walked somewhere in his journeyings. He saw the solemn passages, the penetrating shafts of light, the obscure altar rising dimly in the star-hung alcove; and from the glamour round the altar floated down a magnificent angel, and with a look of perfect knowledge in his eyes shamed him for his base resolve. Slowly, as Louis quailed before him, he dwindled, shimmering in the glory shaken from his vesture, until he grew very faint and indistinct, and dissolved slowly into light. Then his vision swayed aside, and he saw his own gallery, and a little cream-colored dog, that sat with his back half-turned towards him, eying him over his shoulder. Superstitious Louis shuddered when he saw this dog. He thought there was something uncanny about him; but to a casual observer he was an ordinary dog of mixed blood. He had a sharp nose and ears, piercing eyes, straight, cream-colored hair rather white upon the breast, and a tail curled down upon his back. He was a small dog; an intense nervousness animated his every movement.

Louis was afraid to drive him away, and so long as he saw him he could not forget his dream and the reproof he had had from heaven; gradually he came to believe the animal was a spirit in canine form. His reasons for this were that the dog never slept, or at least never seemed to sleep. All day long he followed Louis about. If he dozed in his chair the dog laid his nose between his paws and watched him. If he woke at night his eyes burned in the darkness. Again, he never seemed to eat anything, and he was never heard to utter a sound.

Louis, half-afraid of him, gave him a name; he called him Fidele. He also tried to coax him, but to no purpose. The dog never approached him except when he went to sleep; then he would move nearer to him. At last he got greater confidence; and Louis awoke from a doze one day to find him gnawing his wooden leg. He tried to frighten him off; but Fidele had acquired the habit and stuck to it. Whenever Louis would fall asleep, Fidele would approach him softly and chew his leg. Perhaps it was the soft tremor that was imparted to his fleshy leg from the gnawing of the wooden one; but Louis never slept more soundly than when this was progressing. He saw, however, with dismay, his hickory support vanishing, and to avoid wasting his money on wooden legs he covered the one he had with brass-headed tacks. In the end the dog came to be a sort of conscience for him. He could never look at his piercing eyes without thinking of the way he had been warned.

To pay for his recklessness Louis had to live on a pittance for years; just enough to keep himself alive. He might have lost his taste for gambling, through this rigor, and his temptation to use his master's money might never have returned; but in his lottery business he had made a confidant of one of the messengers of the Bardé Bank. The fellow's name was Jacques Potvin. He was full of dissimulation; he loved a lie for its own sake; he devoured the simple character of Louis Bois. Whenever they met, Louis was treated to a flushed account of all sorts of escapades, – thousands made in a night – tens of thousands by a pen-stroke.

At last, as a crowning success, Jacques Potvin himself had won a thousand dollars in a drawing that Louis could not participate in. This was galling. To have that money lying idle; never to hear from his master Rioux, who was probably dead, and to see chance after chance slip by him. He gave his trouble to Potvin! Potvin took the weight lightly and threw it over his shoulder:

"Bah!" he said. "If I had that money under my fingers, I would be a rich man before the year was out."

The fever was in Louis' blood again. He tossed a sleepless night, and then resolved desperately. He shut Fidele up in the attic, and went off and bought a ticket with his master's money. When he came back from the bank, the first thing he saw was Fidele seated in one of the dormer-windows, watching him. It would be six months before he could get any news of his venture; six months of Fidele and an accusing conscience.

Half the time was scarcely over when, to his horror and joy, came a letter from his master. It was dated at Rio. He was on his way home; he would arrive in about six months. The probable failure of his scheme gave Louis agony now. He would have to face his master, who would arrive at Christmas if his plans were discharged, with a rifled bank account. On the other hand, if he should be successful! – Oh! that gold, how it haunted him!

One night, on the eve of his expectation, Louis fell asleep as he was cooking his supper. He slept long, and when he awoke his stove was red-hot. He started up, staring at something figured on the red stove door.

It was only the number of the stove, but it was also the number of his ticket. He waited, after that, in perfect serenity, and when his notice came he opened it with calmness. He had won the seventy-five-thousand-dollar prize.

He went off hot foot to Potvin.

"Of course," he said, "I'll have them send it to the Bardé Bank."

"Just keep cool," said Potvin. "Of course you'll do nothing of the sort."

"But why?"

"Why? Wait and see. The Imperial Bank is safe enough for you."

Louis had the money sent to the Imperial Bank.

A short time after this, when Louis passed the Bardé Bank, a crowd of people were besieging the doors and reading the placards; the Bank had suspended payment. The shrewdness of Potvin had saved his seventy-five thousand.

When he next met Jacques, he hugged him to his heart. Jacques laid his finger on his nose:

"Deeper still," he said. "I know, I *know* that the Imperial itself is totterish. This affair of the Bardés has made things shaky; see? Everything is on three legs. If I were you, now; if *I* were you, I'd just draw that seventy-five thousand dollars and lay it away in a strong-box till this blows over."

"But," said Louis, in a panic, "I have no strong-box."

"But *I* have," said Jacques.

Louis laid his hands on his shoulders, and could have wept.

Christmas passed, but no sign of Hugo Armand Theophile. But the second week in January brought a letter, two days old, from New York. Rioux would be in Viger in a week at the latest. Louis was in great spirits. He planned a surprise for his master. He went off to find Jacques Potvin, but Jacques was not to be found.

Louis arranged that Jacques was to meet him at a tavern called "The Blue Bells" the next day.

"But," said Jacques, when they met, "this is absurd. What do you want the money for?"

"Never mind, I want it, that's all."

"But think; seventy-five thousand dollars!"

"I want it for a few days. Just the money – myself – I – is it not mine?"

Some one in the next compartment rose, and put his ear to the partition. The voices were low, but he could hear them well. Listening intently, his eyes seemed to sink into his head, and burn there darkly.

"Well, so it is," concluded Jacques. "I will get it for you. But we'll have to do the thing quietly, very quietly. I'll drive out to Viger to-morrow night, say. I'll meet you at that vacant field next the church, at eleven, and the money will be there."

The listener in the next compartment withdrew hastily, and mingled with the crowd at the bar. That night he wandered out to Viger. He observed the church and the vacant lot, and saw that there were here and there hollows under the sidewalk, where a man might crouch.

He afterward wandered about for a while, and found himself in front of the old farm-house. A side window of the second story was filled with the flicker of a fire. A ladder leaned against the wall and ran up past the window. He hesitated whether to ascend the gallery-steps or the ladder. He chose the ladder. With his foot on the lowest rung, he said:

"If I hadn't this little scheme on hand I would go in, but —"

He went up the ladder and looked in at the window. Louis Bois was asleep before the fire. Fidele lay by his side. The man caught the dog's eye.

Louis woke nervously, and saw a figure at the window. The only thing he discerned distinctly was a white sort of cap. In his sudden fear, seeking something to throw, he touched Fidele, and without thinking, he hurled him full at the man.

The dog's body broke the old sash and crashed through the glass. The fellow vanished. When Louis had regained his courage, he let Fidele in. There was not a scratch on him. He lay down about ten yards from Louis, and looked at him fixedly.

The old soldier had no sleep that night, and no peace the next day.

The next night was wild. Louis looked from his window. The moon was shining brightly on the icy fields that glared with as white a radiance; over the polished surface drifted loose masses of snow, and clouds rushed across the moon.

He took his cloak, his stick, and a dirk-knife, and locking Fidele in, started forth. A few moments after he reached the rendezvous, Jacques drove up in a berlin.

"Here it is," Jacques said, pressing a box into his hands, "the key that hangs there will open it. I must be off. Be careful!"

Jacques whirled away in the wind. There was not a soul to be seen. Louis clutched his knife, and turned toward home. He had not left the church very far behind, when he thought he heard something moving. A cloud obscured the moon. A figure leaned out from under the sidewalk and observed him. A moment later it sprang upon the pathway and leaped forward.

Louis was sure some one was there; half looking round, he made a swipe in the air with his knife. It encountered something. Looking round fairly he saw a man with a whitish cap stagger off the sidewalk and fall in the snow.

Hurrying on, he looked back a moment later, and saw the figure of the man, receding, making with incredible swiftness across the vacant space.

Louis once out of sight, the man doubled with the rapidity of a wounded beast, and after plunging through side-streets was again in front of the farm-house. He ascended the ladder with some difficulty, and entered the room by the window. Where he expected to find his faithful steward, there was only a white dog that neither moved nor barked, and that watched him fixedly as he fell, huddled and fainting, on the bunk.

A few minutes later Louis reached home. The sickness of fear possessed him. He staggered into the room and sat before the fire, trying to control himself. When he was calmer, he found himself clutching the box. He threw off his cloak and took the key to fit it into the lock. The key was too large. In vain he fussed and turned – it would not go in. He shook the box; nothing rattled or moved. A horrid suspicion crossed his mind. What if Jacques had stolen the money! What if there was nothing in the box!

He seized the poker in a frenzy and beat the box open. It was empty – empty – empty!

His hand went round in it mechanically, while he gazed, wild with conjecture. Then, with an oath he flung the box on the fire and turned away. The disturbed brands shot a glow into every part of the room, and Louis saw by one flash a gray Persian-lamb cap, which he recognized, lying on the floor. By the next, he saw the head, from which it had rolled, pillowed on his bunk.

He tried to utter a cry, but sank into his chair stricken dumb; for death had not yet softened the lines of desperate cunning on the face, which, in spite of the scars of a wild life, he recognized as that of Hugo Armand Theophile Rioux.

The look of that cap as he had seen it through the window; the glimpse he had of it a few minutes ago, when he swept his knife back through the air; the face of his master – dead; the thought of himself, duped and robbed, fixed him in his chair, where he hung half-lifeless.

Everything reeled before him, but in a dull glare he saw Fidele, his nose between his extended paws, and his eyes fixed keenly upon him. They seemed to pierce him to the soul, until their gleam, which had followed him for so many years, faded out with all the familiar lines and corners of his room, engulfed in one intense, palpitating light.

The people who broke open the house saw the unexplained tragedy of the Seigniory, but they did not find Fidele, nor was he ever seen again.

Josephine Labrosse

"JOSEPHINE," SAID Madame Labrosse, quietly, through her tears – "Josephine, we must set up a little shop."

Said Josephine, with a movement of despair, "Every one sets up a little shop."

"True, and what every one does we must do."

"But not every one succeeds, and ours would be a very little shop."

"There are some other things we could do."

"Mamma," said Josephine, "do not dare! Let us set up a little shop."

And accordingly the front room was cleared out and transformed. What care they took! How clean it all was when they were at last ready for customers, even to a diminutive sign.

"My daughter, who will wait?" asked Madame Labrosse.

"I will wait," answered Josephine, and she hung her bird in the window, put the door ajar, and waited.

That was in the early summer, before the Blanche had forgotten its spring song.

"Mother," said Josephine, "we belong to the people who do not succeed."

"True!" replied Madame Labrosse, disconsolately. "But we must live, and there is the mother," and she cast her eyes to the corner where her own mother sat, drawing at her pipe, so dark and withered as to look like a piece of punk that had caught fire and was going off in smoke. "But there are some things we can do."

"Mamma, do not *dare!*"

But this time Madame Labrosse dared, and she put on her cloak and went into the city. When she came back her face was radiant, but Josephine cried herself to sleep that night.

All this was in the early March, before the Blanche had learned its spring song.

In truth, if the shopkeeping had been a failure, was it the fault of Josephine or Madame Labrosse? Their window was brighter than other shop-windows, and one would have thought that people would have come in, if only to look at the sweet eyes of Josephine and hear her bird sing. But, no! In vain for months had the candy hearts and the red-and-white walking-sticks hung in the window. It was the crumble and crash of one of these same walking-sticks that had startled Josephine into the confession that the shop was not a success. In vain had Madame Labrosse placed steaming plates of pork and beans in the window. Their savor only went up and rested in beads on the pane, making a veil behind which they could stiffen and grow cold in protest against an unappreciative public. In vain had she made *latire* golden-brown, crisp, and delicate; it only grew mealy and unresisting, and Josephine was in danger of utterly spoiling her complexion by eating it.

"There must be something wrong with the window," said Madame Labrosse.

"Well, I will walk out and see," said Josephine, and she came sauntering past with as little concern as possible.

"Mother, there is nothing wrong with the window."

"Wait! I will try," said Madame Labrosse, and she in turn came sauntering by. But Josephine had stood in the door, and her mother, chancing first to catch sight of her, lost her view of the window in her surprise at the anxious beauty of her daughter's face.

"Well! mamma."

"Josephine, why did you stand in the door?" asked her mother, kissing her on either cheek.

"But the window?" persisted Josephine.

"Let the fiend fly away with the window!" said her mother; and Josephine's bird, catching the defiance of the accent, burst into a snatch of reckless song.

Now that Madame Labrosse had dared so much, Josephine was not to be outdone, and she commenced to sew. Her mother always went away early in the morning and came back before noon, and one day she caught Josephine sewing. She snatched the work.

"Josephine, do not dare!" When she next found her at work she said nothing, but instead of kissing her cheek, kissed her fingers.

But why was it that trouble seemed never very far away? Josephine sewed so hard that she commenced to take stitches in her side, and of a sudden Madame Labrosse fell sick – so sick that she could not do her work, and Josephine had to go to the city with a message. Her heart beat as she passed the office-doors covered with strange names; her heart stopped beating when she came to the right one. She tapped timidly. Some one called out, "Come in!" and Josephine pushed open the door. There was a sudden stir in the room. The lawyers' clerks looked up, and then tried to go on with their work. A supercilious young man minced forward, and Josephine gave her message. The clerks pretended to write, but the only one who was working wrote Josephine's words into a lease that he was drawing – "the said party of the second part *cannot come*."

When she went away, he leaned over the supercilious young man and asked: "Where did she say she lived?"

"At St. Renard," said the young man; at which every one laughed, except his inquirer. He sat back in his chair, peering through his glasses at the place where Josephine had stood.

St. Renard – St. Renard; was there ever such a saint in the cal-
endar? was there ever such a suburb to the city? When he left
the office he walked as straight home as he could go. He kept
repeating Josephine's words to himself: "My mother, Madame
Labrosse, being sick, cannot come; she lives at" – St. Renard?
No, no; not St. Renard. When he had arrived at the house,
where he had boarded for ten years, he went up to his room,
and did not come down until the next morning. When he had
shut himself in, he commenced to rummage in his trunk, and
at last, after tossing everything about, he gave a cry of joy and
pulled out a flat, thin book. He spread this out on the table
and turned the leaves. On the first page were some verses,
copied by himself. The rest of the book was full of silhouettes,
cut from black paper and pasted on the white. He found a
fragment of this paper, and taking his scissors he commenced
to cut it. It took the form of a face; but, alas! not the face that
was in his mind, and he let it drop in despair. Then he tried
to sleep, but he could not sleep. Through his head kept
running Josephine's message, and he would hesitate at St.
Renard, trying to remember what she had said. At last he
slept and had a dream. He dreamed that he was sailing down
a stream which grew narrower and narrower. At last his boat
stopped amid a tangle of weeds and water-lilies. All around
him on the broad leaves was seated a chorus of frogs, singing
out something at the top of their voices. He listened. Then,
little by little, whatever the word was, it grew more distinct
until one huge fellow opened his mouth and roared out
"Viger!" which brought him wide awake. He repeated the
word aloud, and it echoed in his ears, growing softer and
softer until it grew beautiful enough to fill a place in his
recollections and complete the sentence – "My mother,
Madame Labrosse, being sick, cannot come; she lives at Viger."

The next Sunday, Victor dressed himself with care. He put
on a new *peuce*-velvet coat, which had just come home from
the tailor's, and started for Viger. What he said when he found

Madame Labrosse's he could never distinctly remember. The first impression he received, after a return of consciousness, was of a bird singing very loudly – so loudly that it seemed as if its cage was his head, and that, in addition to singing, it was beating against the bars. He was less nervous the next time he came, and the oftener he came the more he wondered at the sweetness of Josephine's face. At last he grew dumb with admiration.

"He is very quiet, this Victor of yours."

"Mamma!" said Josephine, consciously.

"Does he never say a *word?*"

"Why, yes."

"Now, what does he say?"

"Mamma, how can I remember?"

"Well, try, Josephine."

"He said that now the leaves were on the trees he could not see so far as he used to. That before, he could see our house from the Côte Rouge, but not now."

"Well, and what else?"

"Mamma, how can I remember? He said that the birds had their nests all built now. He said that he wondered if any birds boarded out; that he had boarded out for ten years. Mamma, what are you laughing at? How cruel!"

"My little José, the dear timid one is in love."

"Mamma, with whom?"

"How can I tell? I think he will tell you some day."

But the "some day" seemed to recede; and all the days of May had gone and June had begun, and still Josephine did not know.

Victor grew more timid than ever. Josephine thought a great deal about his silence, and once her mother caught her blushing when he chanced to stir in his chair. She intended to ask her about it, but her memory was completely unhinged by a letter she received. It was evidently written with great labor, and it caused the greatest excitement in the house.

"Mon Dieu!" Madame Labrosse exclaimed, "François Xavier comes to dine to-morrow!" And preparations were at once commenced for the reception of this François Xavier, who was Madame Labrosse's favorite cousin.

His full name was François Xavier Beaugrand de Champagne. He had just come down from his winter's work up the river, and on the morning of the day he was to dine with his cousin he stood leaning against the brick wall of a small hotel in the suburbs. The sunlight was streaming down on him, reflected up from the pavement and back from the house, and he basked in the heat with his eyes half shut. His face was burned to a fiery brown; but as he had just lost his full beard, his chin was a sort of whitish-blue. He was evidently dressed with great care, in a completely new outfit. He appeared as if forced into a suit of dark-brown cloth; on his feet he wore a tight pair of low shoes, with high heels, and red socks; his arms protruded from his coat-sleeves, showing a glimpse of white cuffs and a flash of red underclothes. His necktie was a remarkable arrangement of red and blue silks mixed with brass rings. On his head he wore a large, gum-colored, soft felt hat. He had little gold ear-rings in his ears, and a large ring on his finger. As he leaned against the wall he had thrust his fingers into his pockets, and the sun had eased him into a sort of gloomy doze; for he knew he had to go to Madame Labrosse's for dinner, and he was not entirely willing to leave his pleasures in the first flush of their novelty. He had made arrangements to break away from the restraint early in the evening, which softened his displeasure somewhat; but when his friends came for him he was loath to go.

How beautiful Josephine had grown, how kind that cousin was, and how quickly the time went, – now dinner, now tea; and who is this that comes in after tea? This is Victor Lucier. And who is this that sits so cheerfully, filling half the room with his hugeness? This is François Xavier Beaugrand de Champagne; he has just returned. Just returned! Just returned from where? What right has he to return? Who is this François Xavier, who returns suddenly and fills the whole room? Can it be so? A vague feeling of jealousy springs up in Victor. Can this be the one of Josephine's choosing? Yes, true it is; he calls her José. *José*, just like Madame Labrosse.

But he is going now, and he is very loath to go; but he will be back some day soon, and off he goes. And by and by away goes Madame Labrosse, "just for a moment," she says. They are alone now as they have never been before. Josephine sits with the blood coming into her face, wondering what Victor will say. Victor also wonders what he will say.

Josephine's bird gives a faint, sleepy twitter. They both look up, then he hops down from his perch and pecks at his seed-font. Suddenly he gives a few sharp cries, as if to try his voice. They both start to their feet. Now he commences to sing. What a burst of rapture! In a moment Josephine is in Victor's arms, her cheek is against the velvet coat. Is it her own heart she hears, or is it Victor's? No need of words now. How the bird sings! High and clear he shakes out his song in a passionate burst, as if all his life were for love. And they seem to talk together in sweet unsaid words until he ceases. Now they are seated on the sofa, and Madame Labrosse comes in.

"Josephine!"

"Mamma, how can I help it?" and the tears of joy creep out on her eyelashes.

Suddenly the grandmother, catching sight, through her half-blind eyes, of Victor and Josephine on the sofa, cries out and menaces him with her shrivelled fist, when they all rush upon her with kisses and pacify her with her pipe.

And now, what is this noise that breaks the quiet? It is a wild song from the street, echoing in the room. There is a shout, and a cab draws up at the door. It is François Xavier, returned for the second time. He stands swaying in the middle of the floor. There is a vinous lustre in his eyes. His coat is thrown back from his shoulder. Some one has been dancing on his hat, for it is all crushed and dusty. He mutters the words of the song which the chorus is roaring outside – "C'est dans la vill' de Bytown." Madame Labrosse implores him with words to come some other time. Josephine implores him with her eyes, clinging to Victor, who has his arm around her. But François Xavier stands unimpressed. Suddenly he makes an advance on Josephine, who retreats behind Victor.

"Scoundrel! base one," calls out Victor, "leave the house, or I myself will put you out!" François Xavier gazes for a moment on the little figure peering at him so fiercely through his spectacles. Then, as the chorus lulls for a moment, a smile of childish tenderness mantles all his face, and with the gesture of a father reclaiming his long-lost son he stretches his arms toward Victor. He folds him to his breast, and, lifting him from the floor, despite his struggles he carries him out into the night, where the chorus bursts out anew – "C'est dans la vill' de Bytown."

It is late when Victor at last escapes, and hears them go roaring away as he flees, hatless through the fields to his home. It is still later when he falls asleep, overcome by excitement and the stimulants which have been administered to him; and through his feverish dreams runs the sound of singing, of Josephine's voice, inexpressibly sweet and tender, like the voice of a happy angel, but the song that she sings is – "C'est dans la vill' de Bytown."

The Pedler

H<small>E USED TO</small> come in the early spring-time, when, in sunny hollows, banks of coarse snow lie thawing, shrinking with almost inaudible tinklings, when the upper grass-banks are covered thickly with the film left by the melted snow, when the old leaves about the gray trees are wet and sodden, when the pools lie bare and clear, without grasses, very limpid with snow-water, when the swollen streams rush insolently by, when the grosbeaks try the cedar buds shyly, and a colony of little birds take a sunny tree slope, and sing songs there.

He used to come with the awakening of life in the woods, with the strange cohosh, and the dog-tooth violet, piercing the damp leaf which it would wear as a ruff about its neck in blossom time. He used to come up the road from St. Valérie, trudging heavily, bearing his packs. To most of the Viger people he seemed to appear suddenly in the midst of the street, clothed with power, and surrounded by an attentive crowd of boys, and a whirling fringe of dogs, barking and throwing up dust.

I speak of what has become tradition, for the pedler walks no more up the St. Valérie road, bearing those magical baskets of his.

There was something powerful, compelling, about him; his short, heavy figure, his hair-covered, expressionless face, the quick hands in which he seemed to weigh everything that he touched, his voluminous, indescribable clothes, the great umbrella he carried strapped to his back, the green spectacles that hid his eyes, all these commanded attention. But his powers seemed to lie in those inscrutable guards to his eyes. They were such goggles as are commonly used by threshers, and were bound firmly about his face by a leather lace; with their setting of iron they completely covered his eye-sockets, not permitting a glimpse of those eyes that seemed to glare out of their depths. They seemed never to have been removed, but to have grown there, rooted by time in his cheek-bones.

He carried a large wicker-basket covered with oiled cloth, slung to his shoulder by a strap; in one hand he carried a light stick, in the other a large oval bandbox of black shiny cloth. From the initials "J. F.," which appeared in faded white letters on the bandbox, the village people had christened him Jean-François.

Coming into the village, he stopped in the middle of the road, set his bandbox between his feet, and took the oiled cloth from the basket. He never went from house to house, his customers came to him. He stood there and sold, almost without a word, as calm as a sphinx, and as powerful. There was something compelling about him; the people bought things they did not want, but they had to buy. The goods lay before them, the handkerchiefs, the laces, the jewelry, the little sacred pictures, matches in colored boxes, little cased looking-glasses, combs, mouth-organs, pins, and hair-pins; and over all, this figure with the inscrutable eyes. As he took in the money and made change, he uttered the word, "Good," continually, "good, good." There was something exciting in the way he pronounced that word, something that goaded the hearers into extravagance.

It happened one day in April, when the weather was doubtful and moody, and storms flew low, scattering cold rain, and after that day Jean-François, the pedler, was a shape in memory, a fact no longer. He was blown into the village unwetted by a shower that left the streets untouched, and that went through the northern fields sharply, and lost itself in the far woods. He stopped in front of the post-office. The Widow Laroque slammed her door and went upstairs to peep through the curtain; "these pedlers spoiled trade," she said, and hated them in consequence. Soon a crowd collected; and great talk arose, with laughter and some jostling. Every one tried to see into the basket, those behind stood on tiptoe and asked questions, those in front held the crowd back and tried to look at the goods. The air was full of the staccato of surprise and admiration. The late comers on the edge of the crowd commenced to jostle, and somebody tossed a handful of dust into the air over the group. "What a wretched wind," cried some one, "it blows all ways."

The dust seemed to irritate the pedler, besides, no one had bought anything. He called out sharply, "Buy – buy." He sold two papers of hair-pins, a little brass shrine of La Bonne St. Anne, a colored handkerchief, a horn comb, and a mouth-organ. While these purchases were going on, Henri Lamoureux was eying the little red purses, and fingering a coin in his pocket. The coin was a doubtful one, and he was weighing carefully the chances of passing it. At last he said, carelessly, "How much?" touching the purses. The pedler's answer called out the coin from his pocket; it lay in the man's hand. Henri took the purse and moved hurriedly back. At once the pedler grasped after him, reaching as well as his basket would allow; he caught him by the coat; but Henri's dog darted in, nipped the pedler's leg, and got away, showing his teeth. Lamoureux struggled, the pedler swore; in a moment every one was jostling to get out of the way, wondering what was the matter. As Henri swung his arm around he swept his hand across the pedler's eyes; the shoe-string gave way, and the green goggles fell into the basket. Then a curious change came over the man. He let his enemy go, and stood dazed for a moment; he passed his hand across his eyes, and in that interval of quiet the people saw, where they expected to see flash the two rapacious eyes of their imaginings, only the seared, fleshy seams where those eyes should have been.

That was the vision of a moment, for the pedler, like a fiend in fury, threw up his long arms and cursed in a voice so powerful and sudden that the dismayed crowd shrunk away, clinging to one another and looking over their shoulders at the violent figure. "God have mercy! – Holy St. Anne protect us! – He curses his Baptism!" screamed the women. In a second he was alone; the dog that had assailed him was snarling from under the sidewalk, and the women were in the nearest houses. Henri Lamoureux, in the nearest lane, stood pale, with a stone in his hand. It was only for one moment; in the second, the pedler had gathered his things, blind as he was, had turned his back, and was striding up the street; in the third, one of the sudden storms had gathered the dust at the end of the village and came down with it, driving every one indoors. It shrouded the retreating figure, and a crack of unexpected thunder came like a pistol shot, and then the pelting rain.

Some venturesome souls who looked out when the storm was nearly over, declared they saw, large on the hills, the figure of the pedler, walking enraged in the fringes of the storm. One of these was Henri Lamoureux, who, to this day, has never found the little red purse.

"I would have sworn I had it in this hand when he caught me; but I felt it fly away like a bird."

"But what made the man curse every one so when you just bought that little purse – say that?"

"Well, I know not, do you? Anyway he has my quarter, and he was blind – blind as a stone fence."

"Blind! Not he!" cried the Widow Laroque. "He was the Old Boy himself, I told you – it is always as I say, you see now – it was the old Devil himself."

However that might be, there are yet people in Viger who, when the dust blows, and a sharp storm comes up from the southeast, see the figure of the enraged pedler, large upon the hills, striding violently along the fringes of the storm.

Paul Farlotte

NEAR THE outskirts of Viger, to the west, far away from the Blanche, but having a country outlook of their own, and a glimpse of a shadowy range of hills, stood two houses which would have attracted attention by their contrast, if for no other reason. One was a low cottage, surrounded by a garden, and covered with roses, which formed jalousies for the encircling veranda. The garden was laid out with the care and completeness that told of a master hand. The cottage itself had the air of having been secured from the inroads of time as thoroughly as paint and a nail in the right place at the right time could effect that end. The other was a large gaunt-looking house, narrow and high, with many windows, some of which were boarded up, as if there was no further use for the chambers into which they had once admitted light. Standing on a rough piece of ground it seemed given over to the rudeness of decay. It appeared to have been the intention of its builder to veneer it with brick; but it stood there a wooden shell, discolored by the weather, disjointed by the frost, and with the wind fluttering the rags of tar-paper which had been intended as a protection against the cold, but which now hung in patches and ribbons. But despite this dilapidation it had a sort of martial air about it, and seemed to watch over its embowered companion, warding off tempests and gradually falling to pieces on guard, like a faithful soldier who suffers at his post. In the road, just between the two, stood a beautiful Lombardy poplar. Its shadow fell upon the little cottage in the morning, and travelled across the garden, and in the evening touched the corner of the tall house, and faded out with the sun, only to float there again in the moon-light, or to commence the journey next morning with the dawn. This shadow seemed, with its constant movement, to figure the connection that existed between the two houses.

The garden of the cottage was a marvel; there the finest roses in the parish grew, roses which people came miles to see, and parterres of old-fashioned flowers, the seed of which came from France, and which in consequence seemed to blow with a rarer color and more delicate perfume. This garden was a striking contrast to the stony ground about the neighbor-ing house, where only the commonest weeds grew unre-garded; but its master had been born a gardener, just as another man is born a musician or a poet. There was a super-stition in the village that all he had to do was to put anything, even a dry stick, into the ground, and it would grow. He was the village schoolmaster, and Madame Laroque would remark spitefully enough that if Monsieur Paul Farlotte had been as successful in planting knowledge in the heads of his scholars as he was in planting roses in his garden Viger would have been celebrated the world over. But he was born a gardener, not a teacher; and he made the best of the fate which com-pelled him to depend for his living on something he disliked. He looked almost as dry as one of his own hyacinth bulbs; but like it he had life at his heart. He was a very small man, and frail, and looked older than he was. It was strange, but you rarely seemed to see his face; for he was bent with weeding and digging, and it seemed an effort for him to raise his head and look at you with the full glance of his eye. But when he did, you saw the eye was honest and full of light. He was not careful of his personal appearance, clinging to his old garments with a fondness which often laid him open to ridicule, which he was willing to bear for the sake of the comfort of an old pair of shoes, or a hat which had accommodated itself to the irregularities of his head. On the street he wore a curious skirt-coat that seemed to be made of some indestructible material, for he had worn it for years, and might be buried in it. It received an extra brush for Sundays and holidays, and always looked as good as new. He made a quaint picture, as he came down the road from the school. He had a hesitating walk, and constantly stopped and looked behind him; for he always fancied he heard a voice calling him by his name. He would be working in his flower-beds when he would hear it over his shoulder, "Paul;" or when he went to draw water from his well, "Paul;" or when he was reading by his fire, some one calling him softly, "Paul, Paul;" or in the dead of night, when nothing moved in his cottage he would hear it out of the dark, "Paul." So it came to be a sort of companionship for him, this haunting voice; and sometimes one could have seen him in his garden stretch out his hand and smile, as if he were welcoming an invisible guest. Sometimes the guest was not invisible, but took body and shape, and was a real presence; and often Paul was greeted with visions of things that had been, or that would be, and saw figures where, for other eyes, hung only the impalpable air.

He had one other passion besides his garden, and that was Montaigne. He delved in one in the summer, in the other in the winter. With his feet on his stove he would become so absorbed with his author that he would burn his slippers and come to himself disturbed by the smell of the singed leather. He had only one great ambition, that was to return to France to see his mother before she died; and he had for years been trying to save enough money to take the journey. People who did not know him called him stingy, and said the saving for his journey was only a pretext to cover his miserly habits. It was strange, he had been saving for years, and yet he had not saved enough. Whenever anyone would ask him, "Well, Monsieur Farlotte, when do you go to France?" he would answer, "Next year – next year." So when he announced one spring that he was actually going, and when people saw that he was not making his garden with his accustomed care, it became the talk of the village: "Monsieur Farlotte is going to France;" "Monsieur Farlotte has saved enough money, true, true, he is going to France."

His proposed visit gave no one so much pleasure as it gave his neighbors in the gaunt, unkempt house which seemed to watch over his own; and no one would have imagined what a joy it was to Marie St. Denis, the tall girl who was mother to her orphan brothers and sisters, to hear Monsieur Farlotte say, "When I am in France;" for she knew what none of the villagers knew, that, if it had not been for her and her troubles, Monsieur Farlotte would have seen France many years before. How often she would recall the time when her father, who was in the employ of the great match factory near Viger, used to drive about collecting the little paper match-boxes which were made by hundreds of women in the village and the country around; how he had conceived the idea of making a machine in which a strip of paper would go in at one end, and the completed match-boxes would fall out at the other; how he had given up his situation and devoted his whole time and energy to the invention of this machine; how he had failed time and again, but continued with a perseverance which at last became a frantic passion; and how, to keep the family together, her mother, herself, and the children joined that army of workers which was making the match-boxes by hand. She would think of what would have happened to them then if Monsieur Farlotte had not been there with his help, or what would have happened when her mother died, worn out, and her father, overcome with disappointment, gave up his life and his task together, in despair. But whenever she would try to speak of these things Monsieur Farlotte would prevent her with a gesture, "Well, but what would you have me do, – besides, I will go some day, – now who knows, next year, perhaps." So here was the "next year," which she had so longed to see, and Monsieur Farlotte was giving her a daily lecture on how to treat the tulips after they had done flowering, preluding everything he had to say with, "When I am in France," for his heart was already there.

He had two places to visit, one was his old home, the other was the birthplace of his beloved Montaigne. He had often described to Marie the little cottage where he was born, with the vine arbors and the long garden walks, the lilac-bushes, with their cool dark-green leaves, the white eaves where the swallows nested, and the poplar, sentinel over all. "You see," he would say, "I have tried to make this little place like it; and my memory may have played me a trick, but I often fancy myself at home. That poplar and this long walk and the vines on the arbor, – sometimes when I see the tulips by the border I fancy it is all in France."

Marie was going over his scant wardrobe, mending with her skilful fingers, putting a stitch in the trusty old coat, and securing its buttons. She was anxious that Monsieur Farlotte should get a new suit before he went on his journey; but he would not hear to it. "Not a bit of it," he would say, "if I made my appearance in a new suit, they would think I had been making money; and when they would find out that I had not enough to buy cabbage for the soup there would be a disappointment." She could not get him to write that he was coming. "No, no," he would say, "if I do that they will expect me." "Well, and why not, – why not?" "Well, they would think about it, – in ten days Paul comes home, then in five days Paul comes home, and then when I came they would set the dogs on me. No, I will just walk in, – so, – and when they are staring at my old coat I will just sit down in a corner, and my old mother will commence to cry. Oh, I have it all arranged."

So Marie let him have his own way; but she was fixed on

having her way in some things. To save Monsieur Farlotte the heavier work, and allow him to keep his strength for the journey, she would make her brother Guy do the spading in the garden, much to his disgust, and that of Monsieur Farlotte, who would stand by and interfere, taking the spade into his own hands with infinite satisfaction. "See," he would say, "go deeper and turn it over so." And when Guy would dig in his own clumsy way, he would go off in despair, with the words, "God help us, nothing will grow there."

When Monsieur Farlotte insisted on taking his clothes in an old box covered with rawhide, with his initials in brass tacks on the cover, Marie would not consent to it, and made Guy carry off the box without his knowledge and hide it. She had a good tin trunk which had belonged to her mother, which she knew where to find in the attic, and which would contain everything Monsieur Farlotte had to carry. Poor Marie never went into this attic without a shudder, for occupying most of the space was her father's work bench, and that complicated wheel, the model of his invention, which he had tried so hard to perfect, and which stood there like a monument of his failure. She had made Guy promise never to move it, fearing lest he might be tempted to finish what his father had begun, – a fear that was almost an apprehension, so like him was he growing. He was tall and large-boned, with a dark restless eye, set under an overhanging forehead. He had long arms, out of proportion to his height, and he hung his head when he walked. His likeness to his father made him seem a man before his time. He felt himself a man; for he had a good position in the match factory, and was like a father to his little brothers and sisters.

Although the model had always had a strange fascination for him, the lad had kept his promise to his sister, and had never touched the mechanism which had literally taken his father's life. Often when he went into the attic he would stand and gaze at the model and wonder why it had not succeeded, and recall his father bending over his work, with his compass and pencil. But he had a dread of it too, and sometimes would hurry away, afraid lest its fascination would conquer him.

Monsieur Farlotte was to leave as soon as his school closed, but weeks before that he had everything ready, and could enjoy his roses in peace. After school hours he would walk in his garden, to and fro, to and fro, with his hands behind his back, and his eyes upon the ground, meditating; and once in a while he would pause and smile, or look over his shoulder when the haunting voice would call his name. His scholars had commenced to view him with additional interest, now that he was going to take such a prodigious journey; and two or three of them could always be seen peering through the palings, watching him as he walked up and down the path; and Marie would watch him too, and wonder what he would say when he found that his trunk had disappeared. He missed it fully a month before he could expect to start; but he had resolved to pack that very evening.

"But there is plenty of time," remonstrated Marie.

"That's always the way," he answered. "Would you expect me to leave everything until the last moment?"

"But, Monsieur Farlotte, in ten minutes everything goes into the trunk."

"So, and in the same ten minutes something is left out of the trunk, and I am in France, and my shoes are in Viger, that will be the end of it."

So, to pacify him, she had to ask Guy to bring down the trunk from the attic. It was not yet dark there; the sunset threw a great color into the room, touching all the familiar objects with transfiguring light, and giving the shadows a rich depth. Guy saw the model glowing like some magic golden wheel, the metal points upon it gleaming like jewels in the light. As he passed he touched it, and with a musical click something dropped from it. He picked it up: it was one of the little paper match-boxes, but the defect that he remembered to have heard talked of was there. He held it in his hand and examined it; then he pulled it apart and spread it out. "Ah," he said to himself, "the fault was in the cutting." Then he turned the wheel, and one by one the imperfect boxes dropped out, until the strip of paper was exhausted. "But why," – the question rose in his mind, – "why could not that little difficulty be overcome?"

He took the trunk down to Marie, who at last persuaded Monsieur Farlotte to let her pack his clothes in it. He did so with a protestation, "Well, I know how it will be with a fine box like that, some fellow will whip it off when I am looking the other way, and that will be the end of it."

As soon as he could do so without attracting Marie's attention Guy returned to the attic with a lamp. When Marie had finished packing Monsieur Farlotte's wardrobe, she went home to put her children to bed; but when she saw that light in the attic window she nearly fainted from apprehension. When she pushed open the door of that room which she had entered so often with the scant meals she used to bring her father, she saw Guy bending over the model, examining every part of it. "Guy," she said, trying to command her voice, "you have broken your promise." He looked up quickly. "Marie, I am going to find it out – I can understand it – there is just one thing, if I can get that we will make a fortune out of it."

"Guy, don't delude yourself; those were father's words, and day after day I brought him his meals here, when he was too busy even to come downstairs; but nothing came of it, and while he was trying to make a machine for the boxes, we were making them with our fingers. O Guy," she cried, with her voice rising into a sob, "remember those days, remember what Monsieur Farlotte did for us, and what he would have to do again if you lost your place."

"That's all nonsense, Marie. Two weeks will do it, and after that I could send Monsieur Farlotte home with a pocket full of gold."

"Guy, you are making a terrible mistake. That wheel was our curse, and it will follow us if you don't leave it alone. And think of Monsieur Farlotte; if he finds out what you are working at he will not go to France – I know him; he will believe it his duty to stay here and help us, as he did when father was alive. Guy, Guy, listen to me!"

But Guy was bending over the model, absorbed in its labyrinths. In vain did Marie argue with him, try to persuade him, and threaten him; she attempted to lock the attic door and keep him out, but he twisted the lock off, and after that the door was always open. Then she resolved to break the wheel into a thousand pieces; but when she went upstairs, when Guy was away, she could not strike it with the axe she held. It seemed like a human thing that cried out with a hundred tongues against the murder she would do; and she could only sink down sobbing, and pray. Then failing everything else she simulated an interest in the thing, and tried to lead Guy to work at it moderately, and not to give up his whole time to it.

But he seemed to take up his father's passion where he had laid it down. Marie could do nothing with him; and the younger children, at first hanging around the attic door, as if he were their father come back again, gradually ventured into the room, and whispered together as they watched their wrapt and unobservant brother working at his task. Marie's one thought was to devise a means of keeping the fact from Monsieur Farlotte; and she told him blankly that Guy had been sent away on business, and would not be back for six weeks. She hoped that by that time Monsieur Farlotte would be safely started on his journey. But night after night he saw a light in the attic window. In the past years it had been constant there, and he could only connect it with one cause. But he could get no answer from Marie when he asked her the reason; and the next night the distracted girl draped the window so that no ray of light could find its way out into the night. But Monsieur Farlotte was not satisfied; and a few evenings afterwards, as it was growing dusk, he went quietly into the house, and upstairs into the attic. There he saw Guy stretched along the work bench, his head in his hands, using the last light to ponder over a sketch he was making, and beside him, figured very clearly in the thick gold air of the sunset, the form of his father, bending over him, with the old eager, haggard look in his eyes. Monsieur Farlotte watched the two figures for a moment as they glowed in their rich atmosphere; then the apparition turned his head slowly, and warned him away with a motion of his hand.

All night long Monsieur Farlotte walked in his garden, patient and undisturbed, fixing his duty so that nothing could root it out. He found the comfort that comes to those who give up some exceeding deep desire of the heart, and when next morning the market-gardener from St. Valérie, driving by as the matin bell was clanging from St. Joseph's, and seeing the old teacher as if he were taking an early look at his growing roses, asked him, "Well, Monsieur Farlotte, when do you go to France?" he was able to answer cheerfully, "Next year – next year."

Marie could not unfix his determination. "No," he said, "they do not expect me. No one will be disappointed. I am too old to travel. I might be lost in the sea. Until Guy makes his invention we must not be apart."

At first the villagers thought that he was only joking, and that they would some morning wake up and find him gone; but when the holidays came, and when enough time had elapsed for him to make his journey twice over they began to think he was in earnest. When they knew that Guy St. Denis was chained to his father's invention, and when they saw that

Marie and the children had commenced to make match-boxes again, they shook their heads. Some of them at least seemed to understand why Monsieur Farlotte had not gone to France.

But he never repined. He took up his garden again, was as contented as ever, and comforted himself with the wisdom of Montaigne. The people dropped the old question, "When are you going to France?" Only his companion voice called him more loudly, and more often he saw figures in the air that no one else could see.

Early one morning, as he was working in his garden around a growing pear-tree, he fell into a sort of stupor, and sinking down quietly on his knees he leaned against the slender stem for support. He saw a garden much like his own, flooded with the clear sunlight, in the shade of an arbor an old woman in a white cap was leaning back in a wheeled chair, her eyes were closed, she seemed asleep. A young woman was seated beside her holding her hand. Suddenly the old woman smiled, a childish smile, as if she were well pleased. "Paul," she murmured, "Paul, Paul." A moment later her companion started up with a cry; but she did not move, she was silent and tranquil. Then the young woman fell on her knees and wept, hiding her face. But the aged face was inexpressibly calm in the shadow, with the smile lingering upon it, fixed by the deeper sleep into which she had fallen.

Gradually the vision faded away, and Paul Farlotte found himself leaning against his pear-tree, which was almost too young as yet to support his weight. The bell was ringing from St. Joseph's, and had shaken the swallows from their nests in the steeple into the clear air. He heard their cries as they flew into his garden, and he heard the voices of his neighbor children as they played around the house.

Later in the day he told Marie that his mother had died that morning, and she wondered how he knew.

Appendix

The Return

IT WAS AN evening in January. It had been thawing all day, but after sundown the wind had changed, and was bringing a storm-cloud over Viger heavy with snow. The first flakes, as large and as light as moths, were fluttering into the village. It grew colder and colder. The weather-wise thrust their heads into their tuques and glanced at the few stars and at the impenetrable blackness in the north-east and whistled between their teeth, for they knew the signs meant mischief. In Madame Desrocher's cottage the doors were shut, and a fire roared in the great double stove. Thérèse was gathering up the tea things, for that meal was just over. She was singing carelessly, dropping her song, and humming it over, and taking it up full-throated.

> *"Souvenirs du jeune age*
> *Sont graves dans mon coeur,*
> *Et je pense au village,*
> *Pour rever le bonheur."*

Her mother sat knitting in her chair before the fire. She heaved a deep sigh.

"Mon Dieu, Mamma, what is the matter? You sigh as if you had the sins of the whole parish on your shoulders."

"Well, my dear, you are like a bird, always on the wing and always ready for a song. But you are young, and we old people have our troubles."

I know, thought Thérèse, you are thinking of Pierre. "Well, Mamma," she said, "I would not be downhearted; we have plenty of things to make us cheerful, and why not think of them?"

"Yes, so we have; but I would remember this year for ever if it would only bring my poor Pierre back again."

"There, I knew it was Pierre you were thinking of; but do you think he will ever come back, Mamma? Think how long it is since he went away."

"Yes, it is a long time; but then it seems like a day to me; and sometimes I think he must come back."

"I wonder what he would be like if he did come home. He was always wild, that Pierre."

"Yes, but not bad-hearted; there was nothing bad-hearted about Pierre."

"Mamma, Mamma, I have heard you tell the truth about him when you have been angry with his goings-on."

Madame Desrocher looked up incredulously from her knitting and shook her head. Thérèse commenced her singing again; she did not notice when her mother rose and went upstairs, and she sang on, thinking of Pierre, how rough he used to be, and how he would never stay at home, but loved to wander about and sleep out in the fields, like an animal. By-and-bye she took her dishes and went into the kitchen. The storm was rising, and every now and then an eddy of wind around the house corner would shriek, and whistle off into the silence. From the street came the sound of sleigh bells and the shouts of the drivers. There was the soft, long sound of the fire in the room.

Suddenly the street door opened and a man entered. He wore an old blue tuque without a tassel, a rough overcoat bulging about him and drawn together by a leather strap, and

light trousers torn about the ankles. His feet were covered –
but not protected – by a pair of broken boots. Over his shoulder he carried a bundle wrapped in a piece of jute. He had not
endeavoured to announce his arrival, and when he found the
room empty he went over to the fire with the instinct to warm
himself, for he was cold, bitterly cold. He threw his pack on
a wooden settle near the stove, and put one of his feet on the
fire-pan. His face, which was covered with an unkempt beard,
was rather attractive, but he had a look of deep cunning in
his eyes, and the marks of fatigue and dissipation were deeply
trenched upon his cheek. He stood there warming himself
and glancing rapidly about the room, with an eye that lost no
detail of the arrangement.

He found it little changed, but it awoke only a feeling of
bitterness for the comfort of it, when he was so cold. He had
not returned with any love for his old home, but had drifted
there as a ship might put out of the storm into the haven
where she was built, without purpose, except for safety and
temporary shelter. He was evidently careless whether he was
discovered or not, but as the moments passed the desire to
see what he could find became too strong to be resisted, and
he moved over to a large dresser which occupied one corner
of the room. Above it hung several coloured pictures of saints;
there was St. Christopher with his great staff, and St. John
Baptist; there was the divine Christ Himself with His heart
upon His breast. On the shelf of the dresser were some trin-
kets, amongst them a little shrine in brass of the good Ste.
Anne, and a leaden image of St. Anthony of Padua. It had
belonged to him; it had been his chief treasure. How well he
remembered it, and the day he bought it at Ste. Anne de
Beaupré. It had not changed in an atom. There he stood, the
good saint, his mild face beaming on the child which rested
upon the open book in his hand.

He had just pulled out one of the drawers, and his roving
eye had caught sight of some notes and silver in one corner,

when he saw a small photograph which he had not before observed. As he picked it up he recognized the face of his old sweetheart; he muttered her name. With this portrait in his hand he remembered some things he had forgotten so long ago that the memory of them surprised him. He forgot that he was cold and hungry; that he might be discovered.

Suddenly he heard a voice singing in another room. He stopped to listen, and had barely time to put down the picture and return to the stove when Thérèse entered. She half screamed when she saw this burly figure, standing with impudent assurance, in the middle of the room.

"You needn't be frightened, Mademoiselle," he said, with a cunning smile.

"I am not frightened. I am never frightened of tramps," answered Thérèse.

"How do you know I am a tramp?"

"Well, anyone could tell you that. What do you want?"

"I want to warm myself. I'm cold."

"Are you hungry?"

"Well, maybe I am."

"Sit down, and I'll get you something to eat – not there!" – as the man attempted to take her mother's rocking chair, – "here"; placing another chair for him.

While she was gone the man unloosened his belt, and his old coat fell apart. He had that feeling which so often comes to men of his class, who have known better days, when they come into contact with the kitchens of civilization, a feeling mingled of envy, hatred, disgust, and a sort of amusement, as if the occurrence were a passage of comedy in the play. His face wore a dogged expression and he sat there waiting, as he had often waited before. She does not recognize me, he thought, but what do I care? I'll get warm, have a bite, and be off again.

In a moment Thérèse returned with a bowl of milk and a half a loaf of bread. The man took the bowl on his knees and slowly broke the bread into the milk; then he pressed it down and tasted it. Thérèse leaned against the table and watched him. Well, well, she thought, I wonder if Pierre is like that. He had taken a mouthful, when he turned around and said quietly, "This is good, Mademoiselle, it's a year since I've had any bread and milk, but my mother used to give me nutmeg in mine." There was something in the tone of his voice as well as the words he had spoken which suddenly linked him with the human race. A moment before Thérèse had thought of him as a tramp; after she had fed him, he would go and she would sweep over his tracks, scour the chair he had sat upon, and let in the burly January wind to swallow the very air he had breathed. His words gave her mind a sudden shock. She had a vision of the hearth at which this being could have sat, and of the mother who could have studied his palate. The remark had the accent of a request, and she brought the nutmeg and grater. It crossed her mind, – how strange! Mamma has often said that Pierre used to like nutmeg in his bread and milk. She stood and grated the nutmeg into the bowl. The man stirred and tasted until his palate was satisfied. "There," he said.

Just at that moment Madame Desrocher came downstairs. She had the group straight before her. The man glanced up at her. "Thérèse!" she cried. "It's only a hungry tramp, Mamma," said Thérèse. "A tramp, Thérèse, it's – yes – Thérèse – it's Pierre – Pierre – Pierre." She threw herself down beside him with a mighty cry. "It's you, isn't it Pierre?"

"There, Mother, there! You've made me spill the milk on my trousers – they're the best ones I've got," he said, growling it out with a grim smile. He held the bowl high in both hands.

"Do you hear, Thérèse, he called me 'Mother'," cried Madame Desrocher, wildly.

"I didn't know you, Pierre," said Thérèse. "I thought you were a tramp."

"Well, I am a tramp."

"No, no, Pierre," cried Madame Desrocher, "but how wet you are! Your feet are wet, wet. Take off your boots."

"No, I'm all right. I must be off in a minute." He tried to resume his spoon, but his mother took the bowl away from him.

"Off!" she said, with a terrified accent. "Where?"

"Why, anywhere, I'm not particular."

"Pierre, you mustn't go away any more – never again."

"I mustn't, eh!" he said, roughly.

"No, no, I can't let you. You don't know how long we've waited for you."

"I guess it's too late, I'm too hard a ticket. You would not want me around here."

"Wait, Pierre, wait until I get you some warm clothes, and then you'll have something better than bread and milk to eat," said Madame Desrocher eagerly, running up stairs.

"What made you stay away so long, Pierre?" asked Thérèse.

"I don't know, I couldn't help it. I'm not like other people. I have to be on the move."

"But you must get tired."

"Well, yes; but that's not so bad as being in one place. I'd rather be tired, dead tired, than to always be like a tree, in one place. Besides no one wants me here; everyone was down on me, it was always 'that rascal Pierre', if anything went wrong."

He began to enjoy talking and the rare delight of complaining to the well-fed of his kind.

"I've tried that 'being good.' I stayed in a refuge once for two months, but no man could stand that. Everything was tied down, and I got sick of it. An old mate of mine said there was something in our heels that kept us on the move; it may sleep for a while but when it's awake you've got to go."

He was beginning to feel thoroughly warmed by the fire, and he stretched himself comfortably. "Well," he said, "you people have a good time," then he mused awhile.

"You might have it too, Pierre, if you liked," ventured Thérèse.

"How?" he asked.

"Well, you could find plenty to do if you stayed at home!"

"To do!" he cried fiercely, "I don't want anything to do. I hate work. Besides there's no use in working. That's true what that man told me in Chicago. There's no use in working, the men at the top get everything, and we at the bottom get nothing, and so long as you people keep on working, things will be the same."

He was so vehement that poor Thérèse was frightened into silence. But, after this explosion, Pierre began to think that perhaps he might stay; the warmth and light were having an effect upon him, and he felt rested. Madame Desrocher was not long gone and she coaxed Pierre to go upstairs and put on some clean clothes. The moment he was gone, she commenced to bustle about and get something for him to eat.

"We must keep him," she said to Thérèse, excitedly. "We must be good to him and he will stay at home."

"He seems very rough, Mamma," said Thérèse.

"Yes, but wait till you see him in those clean, warm clothes; and he has been a long time from home. Poor Pierre!"

When Pierre came down stairs he looked a different man, and he felt the change himself. His manner seemed less rough. He was clothed in a suit of grey homespun that fitted him loosely. On his feet he wore a pair of shoepacks.

"Those are warm socks," he said, with a grin, "and a good pair of shoepacks."

"Why, Pierre! you look like a prince."

"Did a prince ever wear shoepacks, Mamma?" said Thérèse, gaily. Her mother did not answer her; she spoke to Pierre:

"See, Pierre, come and have some supper."

He sat down at the table, and, as he ate, he began to ask questions about his brothers and sisters and his old friends.

When he had finished, he pulled out his pipe and commenced to cut his tobacco. From his movements, his mother knew that there was something on his mind, but she was afraid to ask him any questions, lest she might break the charm which was gradually bringing him nearer to a resolve to remain at home. There was a shamefast expression on his face, as, with a great show of cleaning and arranging his pipe, he asked if Olivine Charbonneau was still in Viger.

"Yes," said Madame Desrocher, "she is still at home, and what a good girl she is."

Pierre sat and smoked contemplatively; for years he had not had such thoughts as were now passing through his mind. He thought of his old sweetheart, and the promise she had made always to be true, and now he heard his mother telling him that she was a good girl and had waited for him. He was gradually losing sight of his old life, forgetting it; he seemed to be in some pleasant dream. He rose, and went over to the stove. Sitting on the chair, facing its back, with his arms leaning on it, he gazed at the hole in the damper about which the fire played and purred.

Madame Desrocher motioned to Thérèse to go and bring Olivine, and Pierre heard the storm leap in at the door as she went out. If I could see Olivine, he thought, well! but it is too late now. That sound of the storm charging the house jarred his dream. He thought swiftly. Yes, he could stay. He would marry Olivine and settle down. But then the storm would shoulder against the door, and he could hear the clink of the snow as it sprang from the edge of the drift upon the window. Something seemed to be calling him; tapping the pane to attract his attention. His mother watched him, wondering.

Thérèse and Olivine came in so quietly that Pierre never made a move, and Thérèse motioned Olivine to put her hands over his eyes. It was the old, childish play, and with it the years rolled away like mist from the pleasant vale of youth.

"Guess," said Olivine, faintly. Pierre caught her wrists and took her hands away from his eyes. They stood up face to face. Olivine shrank away, Pierre saw that she was afraid of him.

"You needn't be frightened of me," he said.

"Oh, Pierre! you're so different, I didn't think you would be so different."

"Well, there's no use crying," he said, with a roughish tenderness. "I'm a hard lot; I'm nothing but a tramp in clean clothes."

"But you're going to settle down now, Pierre?" asked his mother. "You know every ship has its harbour."

The words somehow attracted him – "every ship has its harbour", kept running in his head.

"Well, well!" he said, "we'll see. I've led a hard life, but —"

He hardly heard the storm now, only the long breath of the fire and the voices around him. He went over to the table, and put his head on his arms. He was tired and sleepy; he remembered he must have walked twenty miles that day in the wet road. He heard the women's voices far away; he thought his mother said, "Every ship has its harbour", and the words soothed him again. Yes, he thought, I'll stay at home now, and I'll marry Olivine; he dozed off. A pleasant picture filled his mind. He remembered a rich farmer who used to drive to mass with his wife, his stout carriage drawn by two fat horses, his many children wedged about him. Yes, he would stay at home and become rich also, and drive to mass, and everyone would take off his hat respectfully. Once the storm disturbed him; he heard it calling and striking the pane, but he heard the words again – "every ship has its harbour" – and they knew by his breathing that he was fast asleep.

"There, do you hear that?" said Madame Desrocher, under her breath. "He's tired, tired; he used to breathe like that when he was a little, little boy."

The girls sat close together and whispered. Olivine glanced every now and then at Pierre's head lying upon his arm. He was breathing loudly and irregularly. Suddenly a panting sound came with his breath. Madame Desrocher was getting uneasy.

"Hush," she said; "it was like me to let him fall asleep where there is a draught from the door."

She took off the shawl she was wearing, went softly to Pierre and put it over his shoulders. She stepped back, but she had disturbed him. From the midst of some horrid dream he rose up with a snarl, clutching the table, glaring down at the floor, and uttering an oath. Madame Desrocher cowered away from him, and the girls ran to her side and held her hands. Pierre did not see them for an instant, and when he glanced at the women timorously crowded together, he sank into his chair and muttered: "I didn't know where I was . . . I thought . . .", then he slouched his head down on the table and pretended to sleep. He heard his mother say: "What was it, Thérèse, what did I do?" She was still trembling. "There, Mother, Pierre was dreaming, he did not know where he was." The girls were frightened and they coaxed Madame Desrocher to go with them into the other room.

Pierre, with his head on the table, simulating sleep, had had a moment to reflect. That oath he had uttered when he was disturbed in his slumbers had thrown him back into his old self, and, as he twitched the shawl off his shoulders and rose to his feet, his face was altered with passion. The effect of the warmth and his physical comfort had vanished. His one idea was to get away. He rose noiselessly. His movements were quick and decided. His thoughts were out on the road. His demon was again mounted, and only the world's end was his desire. He threw on his old overcoat and strapped it in, drew his tuque over his ears, threw his pack upon his shoulder. Then he remembered the money in the dresser. Two steps brought him before the drawer. He opened it; he hesitated. But it was only while the eyelid moves; he had never been a sneak-thief. The next moment he was out in the storm; it was mounting about him wildly, and he plunged into it, and

onward to where the little lights of the village showed the
great gulf of the night, his hand deep down in his pocket,
clutching only the small, leaden image of St. Anthony of
Padua.

When Thérèse and Olivine succeeded in quieting Madame
Desrocher the former returned to the room. Pierre was gone.
Before she could think what to do, her mother, followed by
Olivine, came in.

"Pierre!" cried Madame Desrocher, "Pierre! Where is he,
Olivine? Pierre!" she cried, going to the foot of the stairway.
There was no answer.

"Mamma," said Thérèse, "don't be frightened, Pierre has
only gone to the village to look up some of his old compan-
ions. See he has left his boots and his mittens, and he will be
back again." She pointed to the wet boots and mittens, steaming underneath the stove.

"Yes, do you think so?" answered the old woman, ready to
believe anything, so that it assured her that Pierre would
come back. She sank into her chair and took her knitting
from Thérèse.

"Yes, yes, to be sure," she said simply, gazing at the wet
things. "He has left his boots, he will surely come back."

The explanation satisfied her and she went on with her
knitting. Outside the snow rose above the house in an impenetrable mass, hissing, seething, blown every way with a sound
of shrieking in the blackness above. Madame Desrocher
knitted and rocked. She thought, Yes, my poor Pierre, he will
come back; he will come back again. There was a sound of
bells struggling with the storm. She raised her head and listened. Then she smiled and went on with her knitting.

Coquelicot

DIANE GOSSELIN met Coquelicot for the first time on St. John's eve. She saw approaching a small, black kitten, with all the impudence of youth involved in a bearing as resolute as that of a tiger. He walked straight towards her and she stepped to one side; her eyes looked down upon his strong back; his brilliant green eyes flashed up at her. She put out her hands to him; it was useless, he must surely belong to another. She pursed up her lips to chirrup to him; what folly, he could never be hers. Such a completely perfect black kitten must already have a place of his own in the world. But she loved him with all the extravagance of love at first sight.

She could not restrain herself. She called to him. At the same time she took a step or two; if he did not heed she would go on and never look back. To her joy he turned and followed her with a confident and reckless air. She called to him again, on he came; he had evidently no idea of leaving her. Her heart beat intensely with excitement; she suffered the joy of assured possession, mingled with the timorous uncertainty of probable loss. He was surely hers, this prodigy which paced resolutely behind her, no, he was not hers; someone would appear suddenly and claim him! Buffeted by such thoughts, she first half stopped to catch him up, then half ran for a few yards to be free from the pang of separation. But the black kitten proceeded calmly, as if his mind was fixed.

An observer would have seen in the group simply a little, dark woman, clad quaintly in some fashion of her own devising, glancing every moment over her shoulder at a small and vigorous kitten. But the scene for both actors had a deeper import; it was the first meeting of two spirits, destined for mutual comfort. So they proceeded until Diane stood before her house. There she stooped and caught him up.

"I will call him 'Coquelicot'," she said, behind her closed lips, remembering "Mère Michel" and her cat. Then she paused a moment before opening the door. What if Hector should object? Then she would have to put Coquelicot out on the sidewalk. She kissed his little, black head.

Hector was crouched over a table when she entered his room. He was writing with his shoulders as high as his ears. The strong light from a western window, aflame with the sunset, threw his shadow upon the wall. She put Coquelicot down upon the floor.

"See, Hector, dear, what I have brought," she said timidly. He turned his head, and, seeing nothing, he rose and faced his sister. He fell into his favourite attitude, thrusting the tips of his fingers into his breeches' pockets, and holding his elbows close to his sides. Very tall and as thin as a flail, he looked like shadow rather than substance as he peered down at the stranger.

Coquelicot sat between them, in nothing amazed or perturbed by his surroundings. Diane trembled, wondering what would be the outcome of the inward debate, which would be law to her. Suddenly Hector sniffed, and, without another sound, turned again to his work. Diane caught up Coquelicot, and departed silently, swiftly, joyously. She could interpret these dumb oracles of her brother's, and his action meant, –

"Keep the cat, if you like, but for me I have begun my great work 'The Comparative Jurisprudence,' and let him not disturb me."

Judge of the transformation which even a small, black cat can work in the life of a human being. For years, even from a time before her mother died, Diane Gosselin had been a slave to her brother Hector. Even at the time that Coquelicot arrived, she had not discovered that he had imperfections. She shared his opinion that he was misunderstood; that his powers had been overlooked and belittled; that he had been the victim of a cabal, in which circumstances had joined hands with his rivals to crush him. But they had not succeeded; no!

They might have driven him from the bar, he might no longer be able to go into the courts to follow his calling, but they had not conquered him. He had yet that tremendous plan of a 'Comparative Jurisprudence,' which he would hurl upon his enemies triumphantly, and extinguish them forever. He would talk endlessly and dryly on his eternal subject, inspired by gin and water, which beverage had clapped hands with a weak character to bring Hector Gosselin almost as low as he could fall in this world.

He would have ruined himself entirely, and left his confiding sister without a roof for her head or a sou for her portion, but, by a prudence which seemed to have foreseen events, old 'père' Gosselin had left the small house and his little fortune to Diane; the former so bound that it could not be sold, and the latter in Government bonds that could not be alienated. And so, although Hector had long ago ceased to contribute a cent to the expense of the *ménage*, they managed to exist in comparative comfort. Their little capital produced just six hundred dollars, and by the time Diane had paid her fixed charges, the taxes, and the insurance on the house, there was a trifle over five hundred dollars left. With this she made out very well. She kept Hector looking decent, that is, she patched and repatched his old coat, and, at rare intervals, she purchased a new garment or a pair of shoes, but these seasons were always full of anxiety, for he had to be watched carefully lest he would rush off and pawn his latest acquisition. He had an allowance, which he promptly spent. The boys called him 'The Lizard'. He could be seen darting furtively in and out of the house or trotting along the street, his hands in his breeches' pockets, his sharp elbows jutting far behind his thin back. His bearing was a perpetual shiver, and his face, grey about the nostrils and chin, wore a crafty, and, at the same time, an apologetic expression.

Fancy years spent in the company of this person, who was scarcely an individual, who could not bestow affection, and who did not perceive it in another, whose talk was as vain as the pleadings of a rusty weathercock. Fancy a woman's faith and love beating forever upon this rock, or rather lapping upon this semblance of a rock which was merely shadow, and which vanished to let the wave of love and service pass by.

Diane, specially gifted by nature to give all and receive nothing, still had unfulfilled yearnings for something whose love would flow in upon her in return for her own, something which would nestle and allow itself to be mothered. She hardly had a friend in the village; Hector long ago had driven them all away; no one, except perhaps Hermisdas Godbout, saw anything in her but a little, old maid, who looked as if she had 'words in her mouth,' and who was growing a trifle browner each year. Hermisdas Godbout, who kept a small store next their house, was friendly toward her; he was a giant, enormous in height and bulk, weighing nearly three hundred pounds. His voice was so clanging and tremendous, his roaring laughs so overpowering, that he frightened little Diane.

Into this parched existence, stepped Coquelicot, a perfect cat! He understood Diane as comprehensively and intimately as if her disposition and character had been his perpetual study through years of transformation; and she understood him, at least, she understood him as well as it is possible for a human being to know a cat. To her great and inexpressible joy he showed her plainly that he loved her; he bunted her with his small, black head, rumbled affectionately in the depths of his throat, laid his paw lightly upon her cheek. He changed her life radically, awakening all the dormant playfulness which had lain hidden so long in her nature. He discovered a girlish gaiety, which invented plays for him, because he was a kitten, and demure amiability, which understood his contemplative moods as he grew older.

It was strange and fortunate that these two came together just upon the threshold of Hector's great undertaking, 'The Comparative Jurisprudence'. If it had been otherwise, if Coquelicot had not come, how would Diane have spent those days and nights when her brother was engaged in frantic scribblings, covering reams of paper with incoherent monologue, with platitudes repeated and again repeated until the mass of the whole knew neither beginning nor end? How could she have existed merely warming food and patching clothes for this egoist, whose mania it was to spin nothing from nothingness? She would have lived; yes, she would have believed that those sheets marred in their fairness by grotesque characters, had an immortal life, that, as they lay piled up in the huge old chest which her father had built in the room with his own hands, they were really matters of power and would bring her brother to repute and honour. Coquelicot's presence, in fact, had not banished that belief, it remained in her mind, fixed; but her life beyond it was humanized.

Hermisdas Godbout became at once interested in the new arrival; he offered a clean cracker-box for his bed, and Coquelicot reciprocated by making a sally behind his counter and produced three mice. He kept one eye on the cat, and always seemed to know where he was. On summer evenings when he heard Diane's gnat-like voice imploring heaven for

Coquelicot, or making use of small stratagems to get him home, he would bellow from his verandah: –

"Mademoiselle Gosselin, Monsieur Coquelicot has climbed the telegraph pole across the road, chasing the Lefebres' yellow cat with the black face"; or, from the depths of his shop his terrible voice, making the small objects spring upon the shelves: "Mademoiselle Gosselin, Monsieur Coquelicot is asleep with two blades of catnip under the counter."

Coquelicot's advent and subsequent development had not in any way jarred the complaisance of Hector, who laboured hugely at the 'Comparative Jurisprudence'. Diane studied to keep her companion forever shut out from the room, which had a bright attraction for the cat, with its sunny southern windows, and the view of a strip of sod below maples, out of which birds dropped continually upon the sward. It was only when Hector darted out, leaving the door ajar, that Coquelicot had the chance of making an excursion. It was upon such an occasion that Diane found him seated upon the writing table. He was sitting upon a fresh sheet of the 'Comparative Jurisprudence,' his tail slowly distributing the wet ink into fringes upon the original characters. Diane snatched him, too late; the sheet was ruined! Boldly she tore it up, substituted the one preceding it, and departed into her own domain. What would follow? At noon, with a trembling that was little better than a shudder, she brought Hector his cabbage-soup, fragrant with chives. Her fear was quite needless, the inspired one had gone on unconscious of the raid which had taken place in his absence. All chapters, all paragraphs seemed alike to him. Coquelicot was safe!

As the years went by, and the great chest grew full of manuscript, and Coquelicot began to show that he was old, Diane always timid, apprehensive, and full of the small alarms that storm a loving heart, began to move under a shadow. Her mind went often into the future, she began to live two lives, one that of her ordinary duty, comforted by her cat, one that of a possible future, melancholy when she would have lost him. She was troubled when she saw him growing old; troubled as to the manner and time of his death. She dreamed sometimes that he had been worried by hungry, wolf-eyed dogs, and she often rose up to convince herself by feeling him in his box, and hearing his reassuring purr. She was frequently harassed by Hector in a way which led her to spend long hours in disconsolate musings. The great book was approaching completion, (the chest was nearly full); and she was called upon to decide how it could be published. Hector averred that it was quite useless to ask a publisher to issue such a work. It had ever been the lot of the genius to be thwarted by the publisher, and there was no doubt in his mind that every publisher belonged to the cabal of advocates, judges and miscellaneous persons who had conspired against him. While Diane who had always managed the affairs of the little household, was troubling her brain over some plan to gain the coveted $1,500 which Hector said was necessary, he had formed a plan of his own. He would have been perfectly willing to carry it out then and there, but he felt that he would have to win over Diane, and to this he proceeded cunningly. First he began to enlist her closer sympathy in the 'Comparative Jurisprudence' itself. On certain evenings of the week he would call her into his room, and, as she sat in the shadow with Coquelicot on her lap, he would declaim until his throat cracked like a clarionet played with a weak lip. He would work himself into a woeful frenzy, casting the sheets of manuscript from him in showers. Diane, who already believed sufficiently in the 'Comparative Jurisprudence,' was stunned by the enormous obscurity, by the volume of the sentences, which rolled upon one another like clouds, which never end, and never begin. She laid all the fault of noncomprehension upon herself, and what she called her poor stupid head. Coquelicot would often approach a juster criticism;

drawing himself up into a sitting posture, a shudder would run through his whole frame, ending convulsively in his shoulders, and then he would stiffen his ears, and give a huge yawn, look disconsolately at the floor for a few minutes, and fall to licking himself all over! Upon one occasion when Hector had passed the bounds of his ordinary tone, and ascended into something, which, to Coquelicot, might have sounded like the clamour of many of his enemies, his back sprang into a bow, he bared all his fangs, and spat viciously.

Although she had not been accustomed to share the noon-day bowl of broth with her brother, Diane had now to give up her comfortable meal in the kitchen with Coquelicot perched upon the table, and have her bite with Hector, in the room where he worked, ate, and slept. It was at this meal that he gradually unfolded his fantastical scheme. So little did he understand Diane that he stumbled upon the first step. He could not comprehend a devotion so unalloyed and simple. He indulged in verbose hints, in obscure allusions, when a plain statement would have served his purpose. At length, by a progression of faint and half-defined images, through many days Diane found herself in possession of his thoughts. A sudden picture flashed upon her from these incoherent details. The references to the value of their house, the prob-ability of their comfort in any other abode, the amount of their insurance, the chance of a fire, what they would do if money was paid to them, instances of persons who, in his experience, had succeeded in destroying their property, and obtaining the insurance; all these tangled, seemingly incon-sequent observations at last joined themselves into a propo-sition that thence should the money come for the publishing of the 'Comparative Jurisprudence'.

At first Diane could not adjust her thoughts to this scheme. It seemed to be an easy way out of the difficulty, but she had a horror of it, which pursued her even in dreams. But her aversion had no definite shape, and over against it was the power which Hector had always held over her. This plan of his own making was cast into an iron law; she could not oppose it. After all, what did she need, if she could have Coquelicot; she was a little, leather-faced old maid, and had no other true friend in the world. When he was dead and gone, she could perhaps get another cat! No! she looked at him as he lay, his head upon his outstretched paw, light standing in white blotches on his glossy coat. No! there could never be a second Coquelicot. Sometimes she wished in despair that she might be taken first. It would be easier for Coquelicot; he would not miss her so greatly as she would miss him.

Hector wrote the last word of the 'Comparative Jurisprudence'. It was ended. The great oak chest was full. This latter circumstance determined his labours, for the last word might as cogently have been the first. For two days without his task, in the hazy days of May, he was full of unrest, of futile, eager business, darting hither and thither, sometimes standing at the street corners, in his favourite attitude, his shoulders hunched up to his ears, his eyes puckered with a silly, self-satisfied smile. The boys had never seen 'The Lizard' so active, and they began to clamour after him, and one fiercer than the rest, as he was clearing for home, threw a stone, which struck him on the foot. He hopped along, chattering to himself, afraid to resent the blow. Reaching his door, he put one foot over the threshold, withdrew it, and faced about. He stood a moment, looking reproachfully into the road, then drew himself up indignantly, but, as he heard the voices of the urchins, nearer and nearer, he collapsed suddenly, and stepped into the house.

That day at dinner Hector gave the finishing touch to his plan. Mumbling into his soup-bowl, he said to Diane: –

"And, if something could be destroyed, which one of us loves very much, then no person would have any suspicion, we could rush in to save it at the last moment, and people would hold us back."

Diane did not comprehend, but there was something so insinuating in Hector's eye, glancing over her shoulder toward the window, that she looked around. Coquelicot, unseen by her, had rushed across the floor and leaped up to the sunny window-sill. There he sat, looking dreamfully into the garden. Her heart stopped beating, as if held in a giant's hand. Her head fell down on her breast. She saw nothing but terrible blackness. She comprehended, and fear made her numb. She rose up and stood as if bearing up under an enormous weight. She reached Coquelicot without falling, and carried him to her own room. There she lay for hours, realizing nothing, but in a dumb grief, her beloved cat secure in her arms. At intervals, striving to be free, he would touch her cheek with his tongue. At last she allowed him to go, and lay there alone with no movement of life, with hardly a reflection. She was aroused by the voice of Hermisdas Godbout, bellowing: –

"Mademoiselle Gosselin, Monsieur Coquelicot has had his supper off the remains of the two cat-fish that Lefebres' boy caught in the Blanche, and is crying at the back door." His clanging tone revived her. She realized that she was not without a friend, that there was someone who would care for her cat; whatever might happen to her.

At one o'clock that morning there was a peculiar light in the kitchen of the Gosselin house; it fluttered up with a pale blue flame, and then died down for a moment. A figure that seemed enormously tall sprang toward the door which led to the main part of the house; it lingered there, while the light flickered up from the flames wavering in the corner, and spreading gradually along the floor. The light grew until it discovered the shape of Hector, his face pallid with excitement, his jaw hanging loose with fear. Suddenly the flames, moved by some gathering draft, swirled with a roar and leaped toward him. He vanished.

The slumbering village was soon startled into life. Hermisdas Godbout, aroused from his first sleep, rolled off his low couch, and saw fire breaking through the Gosselin roof beside the chimney. A fitful light, appearing and disappearing at a window in the back room, showed that the fire had made its way into the main part of the house. Above this room Diane slept. The villagers rushed together with hoarse, unnatural shouts, men and women; the men clamouring for water, swinging pails and axes with a terrible energy; the women, half clad, and with eyes staring from pale faces, were huddled together in groups. The first-comers had battered at the door, and Hector, dissimulating, had put his head out of the window to inquire what was the matter. Poor Diane was awakened by his yells, and sprang up terrified. She had fallen asleep, weary with trouble. The wall of her room was hot, smoke began to pour up from a stove-pipe hole in the floor. Hastily huddling on a few garments, she joined a group of women on the sidewalk. They were voluble in sympathy, but she could only wring her hands. With a mighty noise the water carts began to arrive, barrels set upon wheels, filled by pailsful at the Blanche; and the rickety hand engine, dragged by thirty pairs of arms, appeared, clanging its resonant bell. The house had been invaded by more men than it could hold, who were struggling with one another, cursing with excitement, endeavouring to save furniture, but breaking it in the press and confusion. Flying from the upper windows were articles which should have been borne down the stairs, and crashing through all obstacles, appeared at the door a zealous helper, his arms full of pillows! Upon the edge of this confusion danced Hector, gesticulating like a maniac, and shouting until his throat cracked. No one paid the slightest heed to any direction issued by anyone. The enormous voice of Hermisdas Godbout could at intervals be heard bellowing to half a dozen active fellows, who, amid the fall of sparks, had covered his roof with blankets over which they were dashing buckets of water. Gradually the flames had made their way into the hall; the stairway was smoking. At length Hector had got the ear of one man disposed to listen to something but his own voice. Hurriedly this fellow collected five others, and they rushed into the front room; there in the middle of the room, where it had already been moved, was the chest, weighty with the 'Comparative Jurisprudence'. They lifted it to the door; it would not go through; to the window; it would not go through! Old Gosselin had built it in that room with his own hands, and of such dimensions that by no means, short of a breach in the wall, could it be moved out. Suddenly the fire burst through the door leading to the back room, and the men, dropping the chest, with a yell sprang into the open air.

So soon as Hector had insured, as he thought, the safety of the 'Comparative Jurisprudence,' he sought out Diane. Her moment of action in this tragedy had come. She seemed quite beside herself; with a scream she rushed toward the burning house. Her words could be heard above the roar of the flames, and the clamour of excited men.

"Coquelicot, my cat; my dear cat, asleep in the back room, let me save him."

On she rushed, for a moment it seemed that everything, even the fire, withheld its voice and gazed at the little, ineffectual figure, going to destruction to save her cat! Then someone caught her, and, in the silence, thundered Hermisdas Godbout: –

"The poor, little fool has gone daft. Here is Monsieur Coquelicot, she gave him to me last night. Boys, bring her over here."

In the glare of the fire stood the Titan figure of Hermisdas, and, aloft on his shoulder, appeared Coquelicot, seated calm amid the tumult, eyes wide upon the crowd and the light, but moveless as if carved in jet for a temple of the gods. Diane was borne toward her divinity, to all appearance lifeless.

The man whom Hector had instructed to save the impor-tant chest, sought him out, and told him that it could not be moved. He looked toward the house in despair. Already smoke was pouring from the top of the front room windows.

"Come on," he cried. In through the door he went, and a moment later appeared at the window. The smoke blew out from behind him, and through it he scattered the sheets of the 'Comparative Jurisprudence'; they fell down in showers, multitudes of them, covering the ground broadly like the leaves of the horse-chestnut after the first hard frost. Thicker came the smoke, and more tumultuous grew the shower of sheets, until suddenly the rim of the upper casement was ringed with fire. Then, amid a thick outpouring of smoke, one or two fugitive pages fluttered out and down. With a shout for help, three men rushed forward; but the sword of fire at the door waved them back, and the inner draft blew a mass of flames from the window.

At dawn the furious scene was quieted, the discordant noises had ceased. The eternal progress of the universe had brought up the morning stars to look down upon the place where Hector Gosselin and his 'Comparative Jurisprudence' had mingled in ashes. It was hardly a week after when Diane, bearing Coquelicot in her arms, walked into the presence of Hermisdas and the Inspector of the Insurance Company, and told her story. Any payment was out of the question, and the Inspector departed with his forms. But Hermisdas afterwards shook her with his voice: –

"Little fool, why didn't you take the money. I knew it all the time. Didn't I know that 'The Lizard' had set fire to the kitchen, Bah!"

There were other things which Hermisdas did not know, but which appeared to him dimly at times, curious circumstances remembered as if from dreams; or as questions which have but shadow answers. Why had Diane given him Coquelicot that evening? Why did she hurry away afterwards with averted face, never once looking behind, but seeming ever about to turn tremulously? Why was she rushing into danger to save something which she knew was safe? Why? Only Diane could have answered his questions, and Diane was silent. In truth did she ever think upon what she had planned to do to save her cat; what sacrifice she had intended to substitute for that enormous crime of her brother's devising. In a little while, after a few tears, any questionings passed away, like the charcoal and ashes which Coquelicot used to bring back, from the ruin, upon his paws, but which disappeared in the rain of one summer. They lived under the huge shadow of Hermisdas Godbout, to whom Diane, as prudent as her father, willed her little fortune, and the custody of her cat.

But who could think of one deprived of the other. Let us then imagine Diane and Coquelicot growing old together, never to be separated, never to know the half of life gone, one never to live on with the loneliness of remembered affection as of some spirit always present, but ever beyond communion. Or, if this be impossible, let us never think of Diane alone as before the advent of her companion. Let us imagine Coquelicot surviving her through a few years of golden tranquillity, always dignified, benignant, considerate; always reflecting upon ancient fables and fragments of lore otherwise hidden in an Egyptian darkness: always dreaming inconceivable things, until he, too, is gone to his heaven, leaving for a little while upon earth the memory of a perfect cat.

Afterword

BY TRACY WARE

In 1896, Duncan Campbell Scott published *In the Village of Viger* with the Boston firm of Copeland and Day. It was not unusual for a Canadian writer to find an American publisher then: Copeland and Day also published Bliss Carman, Archibald Lampman, and others. Moreover, most of the ten Viger stories had previously appeared in American journals, including seven in the prestigious *Scribner's Magazine*. In the appendix to this edition are two other stories that Scott set in Viger but did not place in the original volume: "The Return," which appeared in *Massey's Magazine* in November 1896, and "Coquelicot," which appeared in the Christmas number of the *Globe* in 1901.

Because it is a subtly constructed book, *In the Village of Viger* is often regarded as the most important work of Canadian short fiction in the years between the three volumes of Thomas Chandler Haliburton's *The Clockmaker* (1836-40) and Stephen Leacock's *Sunshine Sketches of a Little Town* (1912). As a book-length sequence of stories unified by setting, characters, imagery, and themes, *In the Village of Viger* looks forward to such later works as Margaret Laurence's *A Bird in the House* (1970) and Alice Munro's *Who Do You Think You Are?* (1978). We keep reading these works because the stories are interesting in themselves, but also because we feel that the

wholes are greater than the sums of their parts. Whereas
Laurence and Munro depict various stages of one character's
development, Scott relies on our ability to notice that the
concerns of one story are echoed in another, in a structure of
symmetries and contrasts concluding in a story that brings
the sequence to an appropriate resolution. The importance
of Scott's book is not that it influenced later writers, but that
it anticipates them. Reading *Viger* today, we are unlikely to
succumb to what E.K. Brown called "the provincialism of
time," which occurs when contemporary literature is thought
to put the past in shadow.

The main themes of *In the Village of Viger* are the appeal
and the limitations of pastoral beauty, the dangers of oppres-
sive traditions that threaten to stifle the present, and the con-
tinuities and discontinuities between European culture and
the life of a small village. In the decades after Confederation,
it was neither possible nor desirable for the Canadian writer
to break completely with European traditions, and so Scott
does not oppose a New World to an Old World culture.
Indeed, from the Seigniory with "all the ravages of time upon
it" to the St. Denis house that "seemed given over to the rudeness of decay," the very architecture of Viger reveals the irrel-
evance of the Old World/New World opposition. As a civil
servant in the Department of Indian Affairs, Scott might well
have known that Canada was not the "New World" that it
appeared to be. He understood the matter in more complex
terms, as he demonstrates in his "Mermaid Inn" column in
the *Globe* of February 6, 1892:

Once in a while the critics across the water may look per-
plexed and ask our poets what they mean by "timothy," or
some other colloquial term, but in the main we must
depend for local colour on whatever there is of real difference in our manner of looking at the old world with its
changeful beauty.

Accordingly, Scott's clear recognition of the danger of colonial status is balanced by his belief that European traditions, when properly understood and adapted, can sustain Canadian culture. That is not a fashionable attitude today, but it is common to almost all early Canadian writers, and it is still detectable in such later writers as Robertson Davies.

From the opening paragraph of the first story, "The Little Milliner," Scott emphasizes both the pastoral appearance of Viger and one of the forces that threaten its tranquillity:

> It was too true that the city was growing rapidly. As yet its arms were not long enough to embrace the little village of Viger, but before long they would be, and it was not a time that the inhabitants looked forward to with any pleasure. It was not to be wondered at, for few places were more pleasant to live in.

Here is the traditional pastoral opposition between the country and the city. As Raymond Williams argues: "The pull of the idea of the country is towards old ways, human ways, natural ways. The pull of the idea of the city is towards progress, modernisation, development." Scott's ironic strategy is to begin with the opposition, then undermine it. In this opening story, a milliner who arrives from the city is seen as a "benefaction" by everyone except the established Viger milliner, Madame Laroque. Despite their fear of the city, then, the people of Viger are attracted to urban fashions. In addition, the characters in this story are provincial in other ways: the constable in particular is a rustic in the pejorative sense, and his search of the new milliner's house is farcical. Another character, Monsieur Villeblanc, shows the limitations of a colonial attitude when he responds to Madame Laroque's distress in these terms: "In Paris, where I practised my art . . . there were whole rows of tonsorial parlors, and every one had enough to do." "The Little Milliner" does not pursue these themes in depth, but they are echoed elsewhere in the book, and Madame Laroque herself returns in three stories, once as a main character and twice as a caustic commentator.

A confirmation of the ironic aspect of Scott's pastoral may be found in the opening of "Sedan." The street on which Paul Arbique keeps his inn is one "of the pleasantest streets in Viger," for "it seemed to be removed from the rest of the village, to be on the boundaries of Arcadia, the first inlet to its pleasant, dreamy fields." The story is anything but Arcadian. Paul is an alcoholic whose obsession with the Franco-Prussian War (1870-71) leads to his deterioration and death. His wife "knew that he would drink himself to death, as his father had done," and so his family is victimized by its own history, like the Desjardins and other families in the book. Because these families seem fated to repeat the past, Viger seems to have little chance of making its own history. Like Monsieur Villeblanc, the Arbiques play on colonial feelings of inferiority: "The Arbiques considered themselves very much superior to the village people, because they had come from old France." Snobbery turns to delusion when Paul regards a German customer as "the incarnation of hated Prussia," then challenges him to a duel: "Here they will fight – you for your abominable Prussia, I for my beautiful France." But where Charles Desjardin's madness causes his brother and sister to cut themselves off ("we must be the last of our race"), Paul's breakdown is less traumatic. His adopted daughter escapes a bleak life by falling in love with the German, "giving herself to the enemy." The irony of that last phrase aligns our sympathy with the daughter and raises the possibility that history need not be repetitive.

By focusing on the ironic use of pastoral conventions in "The Little Milliner" and "Sedan," we get a sense of the design of the whole sequence. Viger has its comic side, and so the sequence includes such stories of courtship and love as "The Wooing of Monsieur Cuerrier" and "Josephine

Labrosse." Viger also has its tragic side, and so the sequence includes "The Desjardins" and "Sedan." The two sides come together in the concluding story, "Paul Farlotte," which confirms that *In the Village of Viger* is indeed a sequence and not a mere collection.

Scott's larger design is also evident in the recurring image of the bird. Monsieur Cuerrier understands the new milliner's arrival in these terms: "The bird is in its nest." Alexis Girouard says that Cuerrier is "as shy as a bird," and Cuerrier asks his new wife to tell Madame Laroque that "birds fly." Eloise Ruelle flutters "upstairs like a dove flying into a hawk's nest." In "Josephine Labrosse," a pet bird sings recklessly when Josephine's mother is defiant, struggles against its cage at the arrival of the anxious Victor, then sings in "rapture" when Josephine and Victor are united. All these references provide a striking context for "The Bobolink," in which an old man and a blind girl release a caged bird only to find that "From that day their friendship was not untinged by regret; some delicate mist of sorrow seemed to have blurred the glass of memory." The connections between birds and characters have been so intricately established that Scott does not have to state that the old man and the blind girl must be reminded of their own limitations when the bobolink flies away.

In the concluding story, Paul Farlotte's love of Montaigne has none of the harmful consequences of Charles Desjardin's identification with Napoleon or Paul Arbique's obsession with the Franco-Prussian war. Farlotte's other passion is gardening, which is symbolically appropriate in several ways. Because it unites labour and art, the garden is at the very heart of pastoral literature. And just as the pastoral world of Viger is threatened by urban encroachment, so the pleasure that Farlotte enjoys in his garden is disturbed by the obsession with factories and machines in the neighbouring St. Denis home. Furthermore, Farlotte's garden unites life in Viger with European traditions: it consists of roses and "parterres of old-fashioned flowers, the seed of which came from France, and which in consequence seemed to blow with a rarer color and more delicate perfume." He wants to return to France to see his mother before she dies and to visit Montaigne's birthplace, but his compassion for his neighbours keeps him in Viger.

The plot is beautifully foreshadowed in the opening paragraph, in which the shadow of a poplar "seemed, with its constant movement, to figure the connection that existed between the two houses." The shadow falls on Farlotte when Guy St. Denis is infected by his late father's obsessive scheme to invent a machine to make match-boxes for the local match factory. Although Guy repeats the error of his father, and Farlotte realizes that he must help Guy as he had previously helped his father, the story does not end tragically. Instead, Farlotte "found the comfort that comes to those who give up some exceeding deep desire of the heart," and he takes comfort in his garden and in Montaigne. Through Farlotte's charity, Scott suggests that Viger is capable of responding to the changes to which it is vulnerable.

In his introduction to *Canadian Short Stories* (1928), Raymond Knister argued that *In the Village of Viger* is a "perfect flowering of art": "It is work which has had an unobtrusive influence; but it stands out after thirty years as the most satisfyingly individual contribution to the Canadian short story." He then received a letter from his friend Morley Callaghan, which began with these words: "Today I got a copy of the Canadian Stories. I read the Introduction, and *then I read D. C. Scott's story in the book.* What is the matter with you?"

Callaghan would have preferred an anthology that broke decisively with the past: "You had a chance to point the way in that introduction, and you merely arrived at the old values that have been accepted here the last fifty years...." Callaghan lived to receive a similarly cruel treatment from younger writers and critics who also would clear the ground of the past to allow the present to flourish.

Duncan Campbell Scott felt otherwise. As he argued about civilization in "The Tercentenary of Quebec 1608-1908": "Our lives should be blown through and through by historical memories and national ideals, otherwise we live in a fen country without vistas, or in stifling air, like old people in a workhouse."

BY DUNCAN CAMPBELL SCOTT

BIOGRAPHY
John Graves Simcoe (1905)
Walter J. Phillips, R.C.A. (1947)

FICTION
In the Village of Viger (1896)
The Witching of Elspie: A Book of Stories (1923)
*The Circle of Affection and Other Pieces in Prose
and Verse* (1947)
Untitled Novel (1979)

ESSAYS
Poetry and Progress (1922)
*At the Mermaid Inn: Wilfred Campbell,
Archibald Lampman, Duncan Campbell Scott in
'The Globe' 1892-1893* (1979)

LETTERS
*Some Letters of Duncan Campbell Scott, Archibald
Lampman and Others* [ed. A.S. Bourinot] (1959)
More Letters of Duncan Campbell Scott
[ed. A.S. Bourinot] (1960)

The Poet and the Critic: A Literary Correspondence
Between D.C. Scott and E.K. Brown
[ed. Robert L. McDougall] (1983)

POETRY

The Magic House and Other Poems (1893)
Labour and the Angel (1898)
New World Lyrics and Ballads (1905)
Via Borealis (1906)
Lundy's Lane and Other Poems (1916)
Beauty and Life (1921)
The Poems of Duncan Campbell Scott (1926)
The Green Cloister: Later Poems (1935)
Selected Poems of Duncan Campbell Scott
[ed. E.K. Brown] (1951)

POLITICS

The Administration of Indian Affairs in Canada (1931)